DAVID FISHER publis[...] he has become a prolif[...] than 75 works of bot[...] subjects. His books have been bestsellers around the world, including 25 appearances on the *New York Times* list. He currently lives with his wife Laura in New York.

WILL ERRICKSON is a lifelong horror enthusiast and creator of the *Too Much Horror Fiction* blog. With Grady Hendrix in 2017, he co-wrote the Bram Stoker Award-winning *Paperbacks from Hell*, which featured many books from his personal collection. Will resides in Portland, Oregon, with his wife Ashley and his ever-growing library of vintage horror paperbacks.

Cover: The cover reproduces the art from the first edition, published by G. P. Putnam's Sons in 1976. The illustration is by Lydia Rosier.

THE
PACK

DAVID FISHER

With a new introduction by
WILL ERRICKSON

VALANCOURT BOOKS

The Pack by David Fisher
Originally published by G. P. Putnam's Sons in 1976

Published by Valancourt Books, Richmond, Virginia
http://www.valancourtbooks.com

ISBN 978-1-948405-52-2 (*paperback*)
Also available as an electronic book.

Cover design by M. S. Corley
Set in Dante MT

INTRODUCTION

Horror has long been plagued by the animal kingdom gone amuck. Nothing supernatural was needed to terrify readers and moviegoers; nature was primed and ready, red in tooth and claw. In a way, the genre's modern era began with crazed birds, rats, and sharks, then bees, bears, piranha, bats, rabbits, alligators, frogs, crabs, ants, roaches, worms—all creatures great and small, as James Herriot would put it—revolting against us hapless humans, often consuming us in the bargain. Suddenly we were back on the food chain.

But worst of all, a taboo of sorts, was when the dogs turned against us. Man's best friend! Companion and assistant! Leading us to children trapped down wells and men behind curtains. Exhibit A: the novel you now hold in your hands. *The Pack* features these beloved family pets, left to their own devices and driven mad by hunger, viciously turning on us two-footed traitors. We deserved it. The origin of this taut thriller, recalls author David Fisher, comes from his seeing signs stating "Do Not Abandon Animals" when he was living on Fire Island in the Seventies. This shocked him; who could *do* such a thing? Apparently vacationers would often leave behind their temporary animal companions before heading back to wherever home was. How could we be so heartless? Several dog attacks on nearby Long Island around the same time solidified Fisher's belief that there was a story there, while the massive popularity of then-current *Jaws* didn't escape his notice either. Thus was Fisher's first novel born.

Published in hardcover by G.P. Putnam's Sons in June 1976, *The Pack* was adorned by a dust jacket that featured feral-eyed canine monsters more like werewolves than the family pets that appear in the novel. Ballantine issued the paperback edition in January 1977, this time with German Shepherds attacking an ax-wielding man that bears no little resemblance to manly Seventies actor Joe Don Baker, who would soon star in the movie adaptation. "The covers made no difference to me, although I preferred the paperback," Fisher remembers. "I was just thrilled it was published!"

That movie version was released in November 1977 (alternately known, depending on the print, as both *The Pack* and *The Long Dark Night*). Fisher was in London when it played at a film festival, and he invited some friends and his agent to see it with him. Ten minutes in and the agent left so fast he tripped over Fisher's feet. "There's a good movie in there," Fisher says of the novel, unsure as to why so many changes were made for the adaptation. But the money he got for it paid for a house on Fire Island. Years later it was discovered someone owned a thousand copies of the movie and was selling them illegally out of their garage. "Anyone who owns a thousand copies of that movie should not be incarcerated," Fisher told an attorney for Warner Brothers, "he should be institutionalized."

With few wasted or extraneous moments and a palpable mood of doom hovering above, the cinematic nature of the novel itself fits neatly into the grimmer side of 1970s entertainments, popular action thrillers especially. Think Warren Oates driving dusty roads with Alfredo Garcia's head in his car trunk; Burt Reynolds, Ned Beatty, and the gang paddling down a raging river; Gene Hackman shooting both bad guys and fellow cops in the back; Charles Bronson putting street crooks on blast. The dire "under siege" scenario Fisher has envisioned hearkens back to various Westerns but also to *Night of the Living Dead*. The novel's pedigree is top-notch.

But *The Pack* can still be seen as a horror novel despite its similarities to other genres. Horror editor, author, and critic Douglas E. Winter has famously (well, famously to somebody like me) written that horror is not a genre; it is an emotion. While that may seem a parsing too far—we *know* horror is a genre, we can see the sign on the bookstore shelves and on our streaming devices—Winter's observation bears an important truth (even a heretical truth, Winter specifies): the *emotion* of horror can be found in a diverse range of writers, from Poe and Lovecraft obviously but also in Hemingway and Dostoevsky, in Carson McCullers and Toni Morrison. *The Pack* fits well alongside other quality "animal attack" novels like *The Rats* by James Herbert, *The Nest* by Gregory A. Douglas, and the novelization of *Jaws 2* by Hank Searls (much different than and far superior to the movie).

And David Fisher has the horror bona fides: he had a friend who worked at Doubleday in the early Seventies; the friend sent Fisher the galleys of a book called *Carrie* by a guy named Stephen King. Fisher had another friend, this one by the name of Brian DePalma, they both went to the same New York health club. In the steam room, Fisher went up to DePalma with the galleys, said "You need to direct this, it'll make you a star." DePalma directed it. Fisher wasn't wrong.

The Pack's opening chapters waste no time in the setup: on fictional Burrows Island, we briefly meet a family at vacation's end, leaving behind the "summer dog" tied up in the woods, where it'll "at least have a chance to survive," rather than taking it back to the city with them. Exit worst people ever. Next up: a growing pack of abandoned dogs, a motley collection too, including an Irish setter, an Airedale, a retriever, a dachshund, a collie, and various shepherds, hiding in the wintry woods, felling squirrel, rabbit, and deer. But as the winter settles in deeper and deeper, the canines have a harder time finding fresh kill; hunger sets in, desperate and gnawing, and they set their sights on the two-legged creatures they share the island with . . .

The island now is populated mostly by old-timers who've lived there for decades; it has become more and more cut off from the mainland, as harsh winters have worn down both the land and its inhabitants. At a city council meeting, several of those weathered year-round residents mention they've noticed dogs "with a purpose" stalking about, strays at the edge of their properties. Long-timer Thomas Hardman is not worried: "Leave these dogs alone and they'll be gone by summer," he tells them. "And no one'll get hurt." Mmm, can you taste the irony? Thomas is more concerned about his visiting son Larry, daughter-in-law Diane, and grandchildren (also Dopey, the family basset hound. You can probably guess what happens to him.)

Fisher wisely, succinctly, reveals the tensions between the in-laws: Larry is concerned that his aging parents will not be able care for themselves on the island as they get older and wants them to come to New York City; Thomas is having none of that. Frieda thinks her son's wife is a cold city woman who looks like a magazine model; Diane is uptight but realizes Frieda resents her since she took her son away from the island. These conflicts will morph and fray and lead to some disastrous results. Even Larry's estranged brother Kenny, a shiftless, womanizing Vietnam vet, will factor into the story, revealing more family wounds and disappointments.

Characters are stubborn, well-meaning but ignorant, set in their ways. These flaws will only make survival that much harder once the family is trapped inside the isolated Hardman home with the dogs trying to break in. Unprepared for the animals' tenacity, Larry begins to take their attacks personally, needing *"to prove that one man is superior to a pack of witless animals, that one human mind can outwit any number of dogs."* After Larry shoots one of the animals, these once-loving, obedient, trustworthy animals are *"released from their early obedience, finally free to hunt every prey."*

What's most striking about this first novel is its assured, no-nonsense, clear-eyed presentation of motivation and event. As someone who's read more dud horror paperbacks than he cares to remember, I was happy to find myself in the hands of someone who had a command of the basic tools of writing. The blunt, almost hard-boiled statements of existential dread I was particularly impressed by. *"Larry refused to look down again but doing so really wasn't necessary. The dog was there. There was no doubt about that. For the rest of his life, the dog would always be there."* You don't get over being trapped in a house by a bunch of mangy curs over a bitter winter night easily.

After *The Pack*, Fisher began a long and prolific career that continues to this day, writing both fiction and nonfiction, with many titles reaching the bestseller charts. No surprise, really, because the talent, control, and conviction on display in his debut novel shows a man who really knows his way around the written word. "I'm happy that people want to go back and revisit my first novel," he says, and I am happy to be the person presenting it to you as part of the *Paperbacks from Hell* series.

WILL ERRICKSON
December 2019

Cave canem

—PETRONIUS

PROLOGUE

It was the second Sunday in September, the final day of the summer rental season. Going-home day. The survivors of the summer's pleasures were piled by the front door, ready for the ferry crossing back to city life. The total was five clothes-crammed suitcases, the black and white twelve-inch Motorola television set that never did get NBC, the cardboard boxes identified in crayon as "household stuff," and filled mainly with pots, pans, and unchipped dishes, the two-grill hibachi cleaned and ready for winter fireplace barbecues, one half-filled carton of still usable children's toys, and the red-tipped begonia that the mother had so carefully nurtured in hopes it might survive the trauma of being transplanted to the apartment.

The father yelled upstairs to the mother, "Everything ready?"

"Everything except for the dog. Go take care of that, okay?" It was not meant to be a question.

Items to be abandoned included five toothbrushes, assorted bathroom supplies, the remains of the green hammock that suffered fatal rips in a July flash rainstorm, six cans of untouched soup, a box of Wheaties, a forgotten carving knife, two lightweight blankets, a bundle of out-grown clothes, a misplaced hairbrush hidden where it fell beneath the couch, and the dog.

The summer dog, this summer's dog, was a mongrel, a mixture of several breeds the most obvious of which was terrier. The children had named him "Jake," after the gray-haired elevator operator in their building. Having been rescued from the dog pound in May, Jake had served summer duty as the children's companion.

The father climbed upstairs and walked into the bedroom. He searched for a cigarette, finally finding an open pack of Marlboros in his wife's cosmetic case. He dreaded this last job of summer, this yearly trek into the woods with the summer dog. "Honey, you sure you don't want to take it back with us? He's really been terrific with the kids."

She was quite sure. Summer dogs made winter pests. They meant walks early in the morning and late in the night, in the cold, in the rain, in the snow, they meant finding a neighbor to feed and walk them on travel weekends, hair on the carpet, checking allergies with guests, shots, smelly kitchens.

But still. The father hated the thought of Jake dying in the winter woods.

"You know," he began hesitantly, "the kids are getting old enough—"

She cut him off. "No, they are not. And I'm not having a dog around to piss on our furniture."

"You don't think we can find someone in the city to take him, do you?" He took a long, nervous drag on his cigarette.

She brushed her long brownish hair, a hundred strokes, always a hundred strokes. "I do not. We'd just end up giving it back to the pound and they'd end up gassing it, which is exactly what they would have done if we hadn't come along." Twenty-one, twenty-two, she created her own rhythm. "So would you please take it into the woods. At least there he has a chance to survive."

"Some chance," the father said just under his breath.

She stopped stroking. "What?"

She knew.

"Nothing." He understood it was useless to fight over the dog. "Okay, I'll bring him out back."

Holding the twelve-foot length of clothesline rope purchased precisely for this purpose in his left hand, he took a kitchen knife and sliced against the grain. The cut left the rope damaged but not severed. It would not be split easily, but constant tugging would cause it to break. It was the dog's hope for survival.

Leaving the rope on the kitchen counter, he walked into the children's room. His two sons had spent their morning brushing and combing Jake, finishing the job by tying a bright blue ribbon around his neck. Jake heard the man coming before he actually saw him and readied himself. His eyes were opened wide, his ears standing taut and back, his mouth forming a half smile. The man meant head scratching, a tug under the chin, or food.

"Say good-bye to Jake, boys, I've got to take him to his new home."

Jake recoiled as the oldest boy grasped him tightly. Too tightly. The dog tried to squirm free.

"Can't we take him back with us?" the youngest son begged. "We'd take care of him, Dad, honest we would."

The older son agreed. "You wouldn't even know he was there. We'd walk him and feed him and wash him and everything."

"I'm sorry, fellas, but we can't. Jake wouldn't be happy in the city. He'd have no place to run, no other dog friends. On the island he'll be free."

"But, Dad. . . ."

"Com'on now, I want you guys to be big boys."

The oldest son hugged the dog even tighter. Jake began to whine. You can't take him," the younger son yelled, "he's mine!"

"Bob-bee!" the father warned in two distinct syllables. "Cut it out! I don't want to see you acting like a baby." Reaching down, he grabbed the dog's collar.

Jake did not understand. His place, he knew from experience, was with the children. The man often fed

15

him, though, so he didn't fight when the rope was tied to his collar, although it had never been done before, and he willingly marched behind as the man led him toward the woods. But as they walked deeper and deeper into the brush, he began to pull back slightly. The woods were dark and too far from the safety of the house. He began to feel fear. He tugged on the rope, but the man pulled harder and the collar tightened around his neck. Frightened now, he dug his hind legs into the ground. Still the man persisted, deeper into the woods, deeper than he had ever been before.

Finally they stopped in a clearing. The man knotted the rope around a twisted branch, then tugged, hard, three times. The dog could not understand that this was a test, that the man had to be sure it would hold at least until the ferry left.

Jake was reassured when the man bent down and scratched his head, then gave him the usual playful tug underneath his snout. But then the man turned and walked back into the forest.

The dog tried to follow him, but at twelve feet the rope jerked him backward. He tried again. Again the rope stopped him. He listened for sounds, for the man coming back, but instead heard the thrashing of the father moving away.

And, for the first time, he understood he was alone.

The dog pulled desperately on the rope, digging his paws into the ground for the firmest grip, but could not free himself. The collar choked him with each pull, and made it hard for him to breathe. But he did not stop straining. He pulled with all his strength, but still it was not enough. He whined, and the whine turned into a bark, the bark into a howl. He howled as loud as he could, giving voice to his fear and bewilderment.

The man returned to the house, trying not to hear the

cries. They were gradually smothered in the thick green growth, so by the time he reached the house they were barely audible, and then only if there were no other sounds.

The ferry arrived precisely on schedule and was quickly packed with the last of the departing renters. As it pulled away for the final summer crossing the island faded delicately into the early evening mist, left now to its handful of year-round residents.

ONE

The big forest buck sensed their presence early. He moved out into a small clearing and waited, lifting his head to the winter wind, listening for movements. The sounds he heard confused him, a steady motion through the woods, seemingly coming from all sides, surrounding him. Yet the buck stood still, pawing gently at the snow-encrusted earth.

A dry branch snapped nearby to his right and he turned his body full to meet the approaching danger head-on, but in the shadowed forest he could not see his tracker. Instinctively, he shifted his weight onto his rear haunches, making ready to spring.

The forest waited.

The scent of danger became stronger and the sounds, simple stirrings a few seconds ago, became distinct noises. Danger was moving closer to him, moving in on him. Slowly, but with purpose, the buck began moving out of the clearing into the safety of the deeper woods. But the danger was in full motion now, behind him, in front of him, at his sides. It enclosed him, yet he still could see nothing. In one motion he was in full stride, bounding swiftly and surely toward the refuge of the forest.

A dirty brown golden retriever blocked his way. The retriever lifted its snout to show a row of glistening teeth.

A vicious, deep-throated growl spewed from its mouth. The buck crashed to a stop, then turned and retreated. A German shepherd came from the right. A tan Airedale moved in front of him. Quickly the pack closed in, making him cut his stride, forcing him to turn. Three more dogs, a Labrador retriever, an Irish setter, and a second, smaller shepherd emerged howling from the forest.

The song of the pack, the cacophony of frightening noises, confused the buck and robbed him of his instinct. He panicked, ran to his left, found his way blocked by a snarling mongrel, turned, took two, three, four long strides, then abruptly pulled up short.

A filthy, matted collie leaped at his right flank, causing him to turn again. Then the pack closed in for the kill. The chance of escape ceased to exist, the buck would have to stand and fight.

The dogs behind him attacked first, snipping at his hind legs. He turned toward them, tried to spear them with his horns, but they moved too quickly. The turning tired him and he slowed. The Labrador finally managed to dig its teeth deep into the tendons of the left rear leg. The buck shook him off, then turned on him. But before he could set himself the Irish setter caught the same leg, biting deeply, this time holding. The buck could not shake the dog off, and the searing pain brought him to the ground.

The remainder of the pack moved in and began ripping the still struggling buck open.

Larry Hardman hated Bloomingdale's. Detested it, loathed it. "Are you almost finished?" he prodded his wife.

Diane Hardman ignored her husband, picked up a pair of flannel pajamas and examined them carefully.

"I don't know what you need in Bloomingdale's for the island," he said in an irritated voice.

"Warm clothes, darling," she told him, the "darling"

18

being sarcastic. "Very warm clothes, for me, and for the children. You wouldn't want your children to freeze to death on their vacation, would you?"

He admitted she was absolutely right, he would not want his children to freeze to death on vacation. "But somehow my brother and I survived growing up on the island without twenty-six-dollar pajamas from Blooming-dale's." His sarcasm matched her own.

She smiled at him. "I know. Because your mother was a pioneer."

He smiled back at her. "Which you certainly are not."

"That's right, Larry, that's exactly what I'm not. What I am is the conspicuous consumer." Then she went back to her shopping, doing her best to pile up a bill that would make Bloomingdale's proud of her.

The following morning Larry and Diane, he the successful architect, she the former model turned successful hostess-clubwoman, their six-year-old son, Josh, four-year-old daughter, Marcy, and two-year-old basset hound, Dopey, would leave their East Seventy-eighth Street, $650 monthly maintenance cooperative apartment building, their maid, and almost every convenience General Electric and Westinghouse could supply, and catch the 7:48 A.M. Long Island Railroad train to Port Jefferson. At noon they would board the biweekly winter ferry for the trip across the Long Island Sound to Burrows Island, and sometime shortly after two in the afternoon would be settling into the island home of Thomas and Frieda Hardman for a two-week stay. A winter vacation.

And much more. The problem lying between them was more than the trip to the island, it was Thomas and Frieda Hardman. Island settlers, people of good stock, but old. Larry wanted to bring his parents into the city to live. Diane Hardman did not want her in-laws cluttering up her apartment or her life.

It became the prime subject for their nightly dinner argument. "They're old," he would argue. "The island's practically deserted in the winter. There's nobody there to help them if they should need it."

"Except the police department."

"There are no cops on the island. They depend on Suffolk County police, and they're across the Sound."

"In Suffolk County."

"In Suffolk County," he agreed.

"One phone call away."

"And forty minutes in good weather. In bad weather the island's practically isolated."

She argued, "They've lived on that dreary island just about their whole lives. They'd be totally lost in the city."

"Well, you can help them adjust."

"How am I supposed to do that, Larry? Take your father deer hunting in Abercrombie's? I'm sorry, but I've already got two children, one dog, a big apartment and husband to take care of. And I've still got my own life to lead!"

"Oh"—he raised his brows—"is that you taking care of us? And all this time I thought it was that maid I pay a hundred and thirty bucks a week to. I hadn't noticed you'd started cooking and cleaning."

She gave him her best bitch smile, conceding the point.

He kept talking. "You know, you just might learn something from my mother. She's a good, tough old lady."

Diane lifted her carefully manicured fingers and ticked off each of the things she might learn. "Crocheting, knitting, canning, darning socks, mustn't forget darning socks, let's see, that's four."

And responsibility, he thought, but did not add.

Instead he said, "It'd be good for the kids to have their grandparents around."

"It would be better for them to have a place to visit on an island. You know, back to nature and all that. Pass the broccoli, please."

Larry passed the broccoli. "It wouldn't hurt for us to spend some time on the island either. All we do here is pile up possessions."

"Oh, please, Larry, I thought we finished with that a long time ago. I told you, I'm sorry if you're not happy being married to me. I'm sorry if—"

"Why do you take everything I say and twist it around? I never said—"

"Will you let me finish please?" She waited. "Please?" He said nothing. She put her fork down firmly on her plate, her method of indicating she was making a definitive statement. "I'm also sorry that you hate living in the city, but there's nothing I can do about that. I can't clean the air up. I can't get rid of the muggers. Some people are city people, they learn to cope with the problems. Some people are country people, they need to hear bugs screeching at night. I am, Larry, a city person. I break out in poison ivy when I cross the Fifty-ninth Street Bridge. The city is where I belong. I'm one of the exact people for whom you design those tall, insulated, four-seasons air-conditioned palaces.

"Now, if you want to live in a log cabin, if that's what will make you happy, please go right ahead. Don't let me stand in your way. I'm not going to fight you. You have to make yourself happy, Larry. But you'll go without me, and you'll go without the kids. Okay?" End of argument.

Eventually they had reached a compromise. Diane agreed to spend two weeks on the island. During that time Larry would try to talk his parents into moving to Manhattan. If they agreed, they would stay in the guest bedroom for three months. After that, if they decided to stay permanently Larry would find an apartment for them.

And if they refused to leave the island, Larry would never raise the subject again. Ever.

All of which lay behind the afternoon shopping trip to Bloomingdale's and the twenty-six-dollar pajamas. Three pairs only. Let him freeze his dumb ass off, she thought. Lovingly.

Thomas Hardman had aged to resemble his island. Once both had been full with lush excesses, but the passage of hard years had turned them both spare and lean. There was no beauty left to them, the harsh winters had worn them both down to bedrock. The honest look, Burrows Islanders called it. When Thomas Hardman smiled a tight, deep grimace split his face, as the deep gorge split the center of the island, and his permanently windburned face was topped with flowing white hair, to match the snow that covered the island earth.

They were survivors, and in a way the fact of their survival was what held them together.

Thomas Hardman pushed back gently on his wooden chair until it came to rest against the rear wall of the Burrows Island General Store. The blazing fire in the old black Franklin stove played bright shadows across his face. He took an exceptionally long drag on his carved pipe and finally said to the five other men in the room, "Okay, let's finish so we can get home before the storm hits." The monthly meeting of the Burrows Island Permanent Residents Committee was now in session. "What do we got today?"

Ned Stewart said that his wife, Margaret, was drawing up the island shopping list in preparation for her forthcoming trip to the mainland. "Tell your wives to call her with their orders. She said to remind you that meat prices are way up again." The Burrows Island Shopping Cooperative had been in existence two years. Don Curtis had fought it at first, calling it "creeping socialism," but eventually the high food prices brought him in too. Now all six island families belonged.

"How about raising the summer resident tax?" Charlie Cornwall suggested. "It'd give us a little more working cash."

"What's it at now?" George Fleming wanted to know.

"Twenty-five each adult, fifteen for kids," Thomas Hardman told him.

"Thank you, Thomas." George nodded. "Seems to me that's high enough. We got to encourage people to come out here, we can't tax 'em to death."

"Come on George," Charlie Cornwall urged, "a few dollars more isn't gonna hurt."

"Sure it is," George argued, "'specially some of them big Catholic families we get. You got five, six kids, you're talking about over a hundred dollars. This ain't the old days, Charlie, people who got money are flyin' all over the place. The rich ain't scampering out here to play no more."

"But a few dollars. . . ."

"It's a few dollars here, a few dollars there. First thing you know people'll be stayin' home for the summer. Then we won't get no tax at all. We can't be greedy."

"But we haven't raised it since . . . since." He did not know since when.

Thomas Hardman helped him, "Nineteen sixty-six."

". . . since sixty-six."

"People are countin' their dollars close now. . . ."

"Another twenty bucks?"

Thomas Hardman quieted them both down. Eventually it was agreed to place the matter under discussion, which meant that next month they would argue about it again. "What else?"

Before anyone else could raise any new business he relit his pipe and sucked in deeply, savoring the sweet taste of his aged tobacco. The rest of the meeting concerned the routine business of running an isolated, almost deserted island. It was agreed to issue another vehicle permit, this to Ted Goodall, who had decided to buy a small tractor for transportation. That raised the number of motorized vehicles on the island to five, including Thomas Hardman's battered black 1961 Chevrolet coupe. It was suggested that Myra Curtis write a letter to Congressman Biondo from eastern Long Island, asking if they might get some government money to help protect the eroding shoreline. Don Curtis disagreed with the idea, claiming "too much government already," but agreed to let Myra write the letter. It was decided that repair of the wooden sidewalk would have to be put off pending an increase in the committee's budget. And finally, the committee unanimously agreed to purchase two new fire extinguishers for the Burrows Island Winter Volunteer Fire Department. George Fleming by name.

"That all the official business?" Thomas Hardman asked. "Anything else?"

After a few seconds of silence he banged his palm on the top of the barrel-table, adjourning the meeting. With the official meeting over, the more important social meeting began. Ted Goodall went behind the counter and poured each of them a shot glass of his Johnnie Walker supply. Then he served them, leaving the almost half-full bottle on the middle table. "Health," he toasted, lifting his glass high.

"Health," a chorus of voices returned.

"And wealth," Charlie Cornwall added, holding his glass a bit higher, and drawing a big laugh.

"Look at this man, he wants everything," George Fleming exclaimed.

"As long as we're ordering"—Don Curtis held up his glass—"a new Cadillac!"

The monthly meeting gave the men a chance to get

together without their women. It was an opportunity to talk about absolutely anything, make their secret men's plans, and simply get out of their houses. They drank a little and gossiped a lot.

"It's gonna be lonely around here without you guys," Charlie Cornwall said, referring to the mainland trip the Flemings, Curtises, and Goodalls had planned.

"Charlie, you can't wait to get rid of us," Ted Goodall laughed.

"Watch," Don Curtis said, "we'll come back and discover he's crowned himself King of the Island."

"King? Charlie wouldn't settle for king," George Fleming finished. "Emperor, at least!"

"You guys think you're really funny, don't you?" Charlie responded, brushing his hand over his rapidly disappearing short, curly gray hair. "Just wait'll you see what happens when you try to come home after your vacations!"

After the laughter had subsided, and they finished laying plans for a surprise sixty-fifth birthday party for Harriet Fleming, George Fleming casually mentioned that a two-yard-long portion of his wooden fence had been knocked over. "The damn thing was broken off," he explained, "not knocked down the way the wind would do it. Really strange."

Thomas Hardman took a long drag on his pipe, trying to keep it lit.

"Maybe it was Big Ben." Don Curtis tried to joke about the legendary giant grizzly bear that supposedly still lived deep in the forest. He drew an uneasy laugh.

"I'll tell you what it was," Charlie Cornwall said soberly, "it was them dogs. They're edgin' in on us. I found paw prints all over my front yard last week. Right in the yard! First time that's ever happened."

"Come on, Charlie," Thomas Hardman chided. "Dogs don't knock down fences."

Charlie shook his head slightly in friendly disagreement. "Don't know about that, Tom. Animals been known to do some strange things when they get hungry enough. This has been a real stormy winter, and you know well as I do there ain't enough food left in those woods to feed everything living there."

"So the weak animals'll . . ." die, Tom almost finished, but Ned Stewart interrupted him.

"I'll tell you somethin' else," Ned started, and the fact that this unusually private man said anything at all immediately brought him everyone's attention. "Three of them dogs, a small one and two big shepherds, I think they were, they come out of the woods four days ago and just sat on the other side of the gorge staring at my house." Ned Stewart kept his eyes bolted on a chipped board in the wooden floor as he spoke. "It was like they was threatenin' me. They just sat there on their haunches. Not movin', not making a sound, not doin' nothing. It give me the shivers."

Tom tried to turn the story into a joke. "Maybe they just smelled one of Maggie's pies and came to visit." Maggie Stewart was acknowledged as the worst cook on the island. But no one laughed.

"I think we should do something about 'em," Charlie Cornwall said nervously.

"Me too," George Fleming agreed.

Thomas Hardman could see the meeting was beginning to take a dangerous turn. "Now what would you all like to do about a pack of what, ten, maybe fifteen starving dogs?"

"Call the dog catcher," Ted Goodall suggested half-seriously as he poured a second round. "That's his job, isn't it?"

"Yeah, sure." George Fleming chuckled. "He's just about ready to come across the Sound in November and trek through the snow trying to net a pack of strays."

Charlie Cornwall raised his glass and carefully examined the twinkling fire through the Johnnie Walker. "They can't even keep their own streets clean. You expect anybody to care about a few dogs on an almost deserted island. Them dogs are our problem."

"Shoot 'em," Ned Stewart said with uncharacteristic firmness.

"What?" Tom asked, unbelieving.

"I said shoot 'em, Tom." Ned looked up from the floor and stared at Hardman. "If that was your house they was lookin' at, you'd know 'xactly what I'm talking about. Those weren't no regular dogs. There was somethin' strange about those. They had a purpose. We gotta—"

Tom put his glass down. "A purpose! These are dogs!"

Ned Stewart's stare never wavered. "We gotta get them before they get us."

"What are you talking about, 'get'? Ned, you're talking about a bunch of abandoned dogs. Harmless little pets. They're not gonna get anybody. They're a lot more afraid of us than we are of them."

"The dogs are hungry, Tom," Ned Stewart concluded quietly.

"I think he's right," George Fleming agreed. "Why take chances? Let's just get out our guns and go hunt 'em down."

Tom examined his cold pipe as he stood up. Very softly he told them, "I want you men to hear yourselves. A bunch of dogs knock down part of a fence, maybe, and then three of them stare at a house, and you're all ready to call out the army. That doesn't make any sense at all. I always gave you men credit for being smarter than that. You're turning into a pack yourselves." He stopped, using the silence to emphasize his point. "There have been dogs in those woods for a long time. They're abandoned there every fall to either get killed or starved. I'm telling you, we don't have to worry about them, these are domesticated dogs, family pets, they're not wolves. Nature has a way of taking care of animals that can't take care of themselves!"

Thomas Hardman had begun to lose his temper. He was a man still in love with the world God had given him after sixty-seven tough years. He had killed God's creatures only when absolutely necessary, usually for food, once in self-defense. Recently he had laid the first trap of his life, and he had done that because rising food prices forced him to. He had never knowingly pained a harmless animal, and it was not his intention to begin now. "This is really foolish talk," he scolded his neighbors. "That's all we need around here, a bunch of armed old men tramping through' the woods in this weather. Look, leave those dogs alone this winter and they'll be gone by summer. Like always. And no one'll get hurt."

"Maybe Tom is right," George Fleming said, not being a man to hold his own opinion too firmly.

Ted Goodall, self-styled rustic philosopher of the island, finally offered his opinion. "Can't hurt to wait a little while," he told them in his most aristocratic tone. "If they do start trouble then we can get together and kill 'em."

"Ted's right," Tom Hardman followed up quickly. "All we have to do from now on is make sure no more summer people leave their animals when they go home. We'll make them register pets, or we can set some tax, but that's all we have to do."

Charlie Cornwall laughed out loud, a knowing, forced laugh. His family had arrived on the island about the same time the Hardmans had permanently moved in, and Thomas Hardman had been his best friend since the day they met. So Charlie Cornwall could say out loud what everybody else was thinking. "Tom, I believe you could sweet-talk a jackrabbit out of its coat if you wanted." He rose dramatically to his feet next to Hardman. Charlie

Cornwall stood almost six feet and two inches, and towered five inches over Tom Hardman. He looked down upon Tom as he spoke, and in itself that created as much of an effect as his words. "I'm of two minds. I don't think it'd take too much for a few of us to go out there with rifles and shoot up those dogs. Maybe it'd be good for some of us to get out there, and the island wouldn't be losing anything."

Thomas Hardman casually filled his pipe.

"But on the other hand, maybe you're right. We're not young men anymore. Ted"—he turned to Ted Goodall— "you're the youngest here and you're what, fifty-five?"

"Fifty-six."

"Fifty-six." Charlie nodded him a thank you. "Gettin' up there. So now maybe trying to track these dogs ain't such a good idea. I think we're all agreed to waitin'. But, Tom, I want to tell you one thing. You're the fella that talked us into waitin', and if anything should happen, you're gonna be the man we look to."

Thomas Hardman held his friend's glare. He was not a man easily threatened. "You don't have to tell me my responsibility, Charlie. I can figure that out fine, thank you."

It was agreed to raise the problem of the packs officially, if the problem still existed, at the next monthly meeting of the Burrows Island Permanent Residents Committee.

Walking home that afternoon, Thomas Hardman found fresh animal tracks just beyond the gorge that bordered his home.

"Those old fools are gonna hurt somebody," he muttered to his wife that night as she served him dinner.

Frieda Hardman read her husband's moods very well, and understood he was still deeply bothered by the afternoon meeting. "Yes, dear."

"I don't know what's gotten into them, Ned Stewart worst of all. I've never seen any of them act like this before."

She served him an extra portion of home-fried potatoes. Age was what had gotten into them, Frieda knew, the fear of growing old and useless. The need to prove themselves still capable. "Maybe it's just the winter," she suggested. "This year's been as bad as any I remember."

"So?"

"Well, you know. The weather's kept everybody inside, and they're edgy from being cooped up. This gives them something to do." Frieda Hardman was the natural extension of her husband. A quiet, thoughtful woman, she had stood with Thomas through forty-one years of marriage, and never had there been a day when she wondered about the love between them. She decided this would be a good night to open a jar of his favorite summer fruit preserves.

His head paused thoughtfully over his plate. "But dogs? I don't know."

"It could be anything. That pack just happens to be here."

It snowed hard again that night, laying down a new white cover almost four inches deep. In the forest the pack huddled close together for warmth under a giant evergreen that gave them partial protection from the storm. The bones of the buck they had killed and eaten days before lay scattered and mostly hidden under the falling snow. A big German shepherd, the pack leader, managed to trap a rabbit, crushing its skull with the neat force of his strong canines. He permitted the other shepherd in the pack, and the sick terrier mongrel, to share his kill.

But it was not enough, the pack was starving. The rabbit was the last food they would find for two days.

TWO

Burrows Island is an almost forgotten bit of land lying off the eastern tip of Long Island. Although it forms a triangle with Shelter and Gardiners islands, it juts farther out into the Atlantic than either of them, and therefore is not afforded the protection from sweeping winter winds, and the resultant colder weather, that Orient Point naturally provides its neighboring islands. Its winters are long and harsh, and the winds, strong tides, and tricky currents make winter passage across the sound extremely hazardous.

The more protected western side of the island is rounder and wider than the eastern end, which eroding seas have worn almost to a point, so that the island itself vaguely resembles a tear. At one point in recent history, New York State geography books identified the island as "God's Tear," rather than by its historical name.

The larger western section is partially separated from the smaller eastern portion by a geophysical scar in the earth termed the gorge. No deeper than eight to ten feet, the gorge is in some places as wide across as it is deep. Residents have erected numerous wooden foot bridges, so the gorge has been made easy to traverse.

It is believed, but nowhere recorded, that Dutch explorers first landed on the island in the middle 1600s, abandoning it for more protected territory when winter set in. Pirate George Proud supposedly buried part of his great treasure on one of the island beaches while fleeing English men-of-war, and hunting for the legendary millions in gold once brought floods of summer tourists on day trips. But no trace of the treasure has ever been discovered.

During the Revolutionary War a small outpost, too small to be called a fort, was established to monitor British shipping on Long Island Sound, and when an early season storm smashed a British troop ship onto the outside shoals, the colonials fought a short battle with English survivors. Before the redcoats managed their retreat to the mainland in lifeboats they killed twenty-four-year-old Jacob Burrows. At the end of the war the island was officially named after this single fallen soldier.

The island was "rediscovered" in the early 1900s. After it had been left to the care of a few farmers for over a century, the Gatsby crowd turned it into a fashionable summer resort. It was featured in many high-fashion magazines as a hideaway for the rich, and a considerable service population settled there permanently. The evolution of the automobile-for-everyman brought an influx of middle-class vacationers and sent its wealthier residents fleeing the common herd. Then the advent of affordable air travel sent the middle class looking for more exotic spots and gradually the summer tourist trade dissipated. During the winter Burrows Island is inhabited by six permanent resident families, a few forest deer, and some smaller animals.

Burrows Island had begun to die.

From October through February the *Bountiful Islander,* one of the four small ferries that work the island in the summer, crossed the Long Island Sound twice each month, carrying food, mail, and the occasional winter visitor to the island. Although it usually sailed back empty, on its second January voyage almost a full year earlier, it had carried the mortal remains of Nathaniel Resnick, the widower, who died alone and untended, lying where he fell for five full days. His death, at seventy-eight, reduced the island's permanent population to six elderly couples.

There was some talk of cutting down to a single monthly ferry trip through the winter.

Thomas and Frieda Hardman bundled up warmly and drove the '61 Chevy to meet the *Bountiful Islander*. They joined their neighbors on the small dock to send off the three families going to the mainland for vacation and personal repairs, and to pick up their food order. And they joyfully collected their thirty-five-year-old son, Larry, his thirty-three-year-old wife, Diane, the couple's two children and Dopey, the family's basset hound.

Larry and Diane Hardman had not seen his parents since their weekend visit to the island seven months earlier. Larry kissed and held both of them tightly. Diane gave each of them a brush on the cheek. Frieda Hardman smiled as widely as she could and told Diane how welcome she was on the island.

"It's lovely to be back here again, Mrs. Hardman," Diane answered. Small lies were easy.

The children were hugged and held by their grandparents and responded with genuine affection. This island trip was the second biggest adventure of their young lives. The year before Diane had insisted on taking them with her to Paris.

"It's just great seeing you," Larry told his parents as everyone climbed into the Chevy.

"We're glad you're all here," his father responded. Thomas Hardman knew exactly why they had come to Burrows Island, and almost wished they had stayed in their insulated New York apartment. He hated arguing with his oldest son. And, although he felt a twinge of guilt acknowledging it, he simply did not like his daughter-in-law.

"Ma, you look beautiful," Larry said from the backseat.

"You do, Mrs. Hardman," Diane agreed. She had never felt comfortable calling her in-laws by anything but their proper names.

Frieda blushed as a mother is supposed to blush when her son compliments her on her appearance.

"Oh, I'm getting fat," she protested.

"She is not," Tom stated flatly. "I'll bet she doesn't weigh five pounds more than she did the day I married her." He hesitated slightly. "Well, maybe five."

Then there was silence in the car as each of the occupants racked their minds for something to say. Diane finally attempted to break the quiet. "The snow really makes the island look beautiful. I've never seen it in winter."

Tom gently corrected her, "It's beautiful even without the snow."

More silence.

Diane watched as they drove through the heavy woods, occasionally passing a boarded-up summer house. She'd never realized the Hardmans were so isolated. The island seemed so small, yet they had been driving ten minutes without seeing a sign of life.

"I'll just bet you're all starved to death," Frieda finally burst out. "It's going to be so nice to have some real eaters to cook for."

Larry laughed. "What's the matter with Pop?"

"Him?" His mother frowned. "He still doesn't know good food from bad."

Abruptly Dopey began to howl. The dog continued the strange yelping even after Diane shushed him, and she eventually had to slap him hard across his hindquarters to quiet him. But even then he continued to whine softly. "It must be the car," Tom suggested.

"No," Diane said, "he's been in cars before. Usually he loves it." The dog huddled under the front seat and continued whimpering softly.

"Grammie, can you make brownies?" Josh wanted to know, his sole memory of Frieda being of a matronly woman who spent most of her short visit to their apartment in New York standing over the oven baking cookies.

Frieda was about to answer that she would love to bake brownies for him, but Diane interrupted. "Josh, Grandma has enough to do without spending the day cooking for you." Frieda did not bother to protest, never having been a person to push into places where she was not welcome.

The drive from dockside to the edge of the wooden bridge near the house normally took no more than fifteen minutes, but the fresh-fallen snow made the trip unusually difficult and they were in the car nearly twenty-five minutes.

The Hardman house stood on the eastern side of the island, separated from the three-store town and harbor by the forest and gorge. Constructed of wood and stone, completion date uncertain, it stood two stories and an unfinished attic high. The first floor contained the eat-in-kitchen-dining room, a large living room, and a screened-in porch. A carpeted staircase tucked into a living room alcove led to three bedrooms and two baths, and a removable ladder at the rear of the second floor provided access to the attic hatch. There were wood-burning fireplaces in the kitchen, the living room and the upstairs bedroom directly above the kitchen. But the kitchen was the heart of the house, the room in which Frieda and Tom had passed most of their lives. Its windows looked out onto the front yard, the gorge, the edge of the forest, and the wooden fence. It was from this window over the sink that Frieda Hardman had watched her two boys grow to manhood.

The porch, closed off for winter, had been added in 1948, at the same time Tom had installed the second bathroom, but except for those improvements the house stood as originally built. The Hardman family had rented the place for twenty dollars a month when they first arrived on the island, and purchased it outright in 1931 after the owner suffered catastrophic losses in the Great Crash. At one time Tom Hardman had hopes his older son would live there. Now he realized, sadly, that the house would probably die with him.

It was set at the very top of a ridge, the highest piece of land on the island, and on three sides commanded a sweeping view of open fields. On the fourth side, the side viewed from the kitchen window, dense forest reached to the edge of the gorge.

Seen from the kitchen window, the gorge angled by the house from left to right. In winter it normally stayed half full with snow. In spring the melting snow created a trickling brook which by midsummer went dry and dusty.

At the point where it passed closest to the house, the gorge was seven feet wide and varied between five and eight feet deep. When Larry had still been a baby, even before his brother, Kenny, had been born, Tom built a long picket fence alongside the gorge to protect his son. The only access from the yard was a six-foot-wide wooden footbridge that spanned the gorge.

The Hardmans' nearest neighbors were Charlie and Cornelia Cornwall, but their modest house was not even visible from the top of the ridge. It was tucked into a small depression about a mile and a half straight across the fields. By the snow-covered, winding dirt road, it was three miles. And except for this elderly couple, the Hardmans were alone on the eastern half of the island.

As Tom pulled the Chevy to a stop near the footbridge Larry said, as much to himself as to the others in the car, "It's still such a pretty house."

"It looks like a page out of Currier and Ives," Diane added, meaning it as an admiring compliment, but which both Thomas and Frieda interpreted as a reminder of their ages.

Diane had somehow managed to cram all their belongings into two large Vuitton suitcases, an overnight bag and a small cosmetic kit. Although knowing she would have little use for cosmetics during their stay, she carried the baby blue kit as security. Hitching the overnight bag on her shoulder, she picked up the kit and walked across the bridge. Behind her, Tom lifted the heavier suitcase. Larry tried to take it from him. "Let me, Dad."

Tom held on tight. "I can carry it," he said curtly. The bag was heavy, too heavy for him in fact, and he struggled to make it look as if he were not struggling, his mind focused on the weight of the bag, so he did not notice that garbage had been strewn around the edges of the shallow backyard pit in which he buried the nonflammable refuse.

The thing on all their minds, the reason for the visit, was not mentioned that first night. Each of them knew it would have its time, but first the family bonds that time and distance had loosened had to be tightened. Frieda prepared a fine chicken and trimmings dinner, gently reprimanding Diane when she made the half-hearted obligatory offer to help, and the dinner conversation roamed across the years. They gossiped about Larry's old friends, about the island, about his job, about the children.

At appropriate times, Tom remembered growing-up stories.

Diane listened quietly, occasionally asking a question or adding a point, showed proper interest when Tom or Frieda told one of their stories, laughed promptly, and answered the few thoughts specifically directed at her. But during the conversation she decided to have her nails shaped, pondered a new hairstyle, and wondered if the broad smiles of the new man at the salon were merely friendly or had a touch of invitation in them.

"I bumped into Vernon Thomas," Larry suddenly remembered, as if it had been truly important. The

Thomas family had been annual summer visitors during his childhood, Vernon Thomas a casual friend. ". . . on East Fifty-first Street."

"What's he doing with himself?" Tom wanted to know.

Something for the city, Larry explained, something that ended with a good pension and would let him retire at forty-one. But he really couldn't remember exactly what it was that Vernon Thomas said he was doing.

Frieda glanced at her daughter-in-law as Larry spoke. Certainly very pretty, she thought, like a model in the magazines. But cold-looking, so planned, there was no feeling in her prettiness.

"Is he still fat?" Tom asked.

She did not like the way her cheekbones sat so high on her face. Or her rifle-thin nose. And the makeup, makeup at dinner, as if she couldn't exist without all those cosmetics.

"He's not fat anymore," Larry said and laughed. "Now he's just bald."

All of it too fine, too calculated. Diane was not at all the woman Frieda would have wished for her son. Too much a city person. Her son, she truly believed, would always have his heart on the island.

"Have you heard from Kenny lately?" Larry asked about his younger brother.

Diane caught Frieda staring at her. But even as she looked Frieda had moved her eyes back to the men.

Tom sighed. "He's still up in Connecticut. I don't know what he's doing."

"He still has no idea what he wants to do?"

"He wants to have a good time, mostly."

Diane watched as Frieda stood up and went to the worn spot in the tiles directly in front of the sink. She was aware her mother-in-law did not like her, and understood why. It didn't bother her. Larry was her property now, and it was her life with him that mattered.

Tom shrugged his shoulders. Kenny. Kenny had been the greatest disappointment of his life. "He just can't make decisions," he said, and left it at that.

For dessert Frieda served homemade apple pie with one scoop of chocolate ice cream, a pile of real whipped cream and garden-grown cherries on top, thereby winning the loyalty of her grandchildren forever. Diane, counting calories, passed on dessert.

After dinner the children played with Dopey on the round throw rug in the living room as the adults stayed at the wooden table finishing their reminiscences. By ten that night Josh and Marcy were tucked safely into their Bloomingdale flannel pajamas and fast asleep in the rear upstairs bedroom.

Less than an hour later, in the bedroom directly above the kitchen, Larry snuggled close to Diane. The sizzling wood fire Tom had laid filled the room with warmth and light, and darting shadows played their own special games across the walls. Larry lay quietly for a few moments, listening to his wife's steady breathing. They slept with her body curled up inside his, her back to his front. His face was buried in her dark hair, and he breathed its soft smell. After all these years, ten years, he thought, we still fit so well together. Reaching under the top of her pajamas, he slid his hand across her breasts. And began rubbing gently. And felt her warmth move through him. Her breasts were smallish, but round, firm and sensitive. Her nipples turned hard almost as soon as he touched them, and he stroked them easily between his thumb and forefinger.

He pulled himself closer to her and ran his hand down the front of her body, kissing the warmth of the back of her neck.

She stretched languidly, then seemed to reach consciousness, and wiggled free. "Not with your parents . . ." she whispered.

He said nothing, but took his hand out from under her pajamas and held her around the waist, his hand resting gently on her hip. A few minutes later, long enough so it could seem to be free from feelings of rejection, he removed his hand entirely and rolled over onto his left side. They slept the rest of the night back to back in the dying glow of the fire.

The short-haired mongrel terrier that had been briefly named Jake lost his battle on that same night. As the father had hoped on the second Sunday in September, the summer dog had managed to break the rope and gain his freedom within a few hours. Following his senses through the unknown forest, he scampered back toward the house, only to find it locked and empty. He spent his first night outdoors alone, cold, and frightened into immobility, but the second day his cries were heard by the pack and he was searched out. At first he had been afraid of the larger dogs in the pack, but gradually they won his trust. He learned to hunt with them, savoring his first taste of rabbit, squirrel and deer.

The big shepherd had taken charge of him that first day. Jake was the second smallest dog, a dachshund being the smallest, and the leader, sensing his needs, made sure he shared in each kill. But as the snows came the kills had become fewer. Eventually, like the rest of the pack, he learned to eat his own feces.

At night he would curl his small body inside the leader's gray legs for warmth and protection. The relationship was simple; the small dog needing help, the large dog providing it.

It all made no difference though. He was simply too small to survive the rigors of the island winter. Even with enough food the weather would have been too harsh for him, as it was for all the small dogs save the strange dachshund, but he did not have that food. He began having trouble staying with the pack when it moved, and because he moved slowly his blood circulated less and he became colder. On the first night of Larry and Diane Hardman's visit, he curled himself up within the gray shepherd, whined briefly, closed his eyes, and froze to death.

Early the next morning the starving Labrador began gnawing at the body, cracking a frozen leg as it attempted to cannibalize the remains of the small dog. The rest of the pack, except the shepherd, watched as the Labrador tried to tear the mongrel open, but it was too solidly frozen in death and he could not manage to reach the meat.

The shepherd spent its time unsuccessfully searching the area for small game. Eventually the pack drifted into a sluggish hunt, and the edges of the winter storm that hit the mainland buried the mongrel's carcass under clean snow.

Larry and Thomas Hardman passed within twenty yards of the body in midmorning, but by then it was already covered and they did not see it. At first they walked silently, listening to the rhythmic crunch of snowcrust under their boots, each of them waiting for the right moment to begin the inevitable conversation.

Larry finally began. Without looking at his father he said, "You know why we're here, don't you, Dad?"

Thomas Hardman wanted to know the enemy fully before responding to the attack. And then they would meet head-on, no dull-edge hints, no held-back thoughts, no apologies. This was man to man, father to son. When it was finished, and each had said his piece, they would understand each other. Father and son, man to man. "No, son," he lied. "I'm not exactly sure what you mean."

They trudged on, Tom Hardman a step in the lead. Larry pulled up the fur collar of his winter coat, and some wet snow dropped down his back. "I want you and Mom to move back to New York with us."

"Oh, that?" Tom replied in an exaggerated, almost mocking tone. "Son, I thought we about talked that out."

"I know how you feel about this island, Dad, but this time you've got to face facts. There's nobody here who can help you if you get sick or have an accident. There's nobody who can do a single damn thing." It wasn't exactly what Larry had planned to say, less forceful than he had hoped, but it served as a start.

"You're right, son, Burrows is pretty isolated. So I have a suggestion. Since Nat Resnick died last year his place's been boarded up. Why don't you and Diane and the kids move onto the island?" The battle was joined.

Tom Hardman halted and turned to face his son. "The answer is no, Larry," he said harshly. "This is my home. This is where I belong and where your mother belongs, and maybe even where you belong. When I leave here, it'll be like Nat Resnick."

It was exactly the answer Larry expected, exactly what he had readied himself to argue against. No answer at all, just outright stubbornness. "Tell me, Dad, do you really think I'm being selfish wanting you to leave the island? Do you think I'd be better off if you were in New York? I don't understand, why do you blame me for wanting you to live longer? Please tell me, because I don't understand."

Tom Hardman rolled his tongue around his lips, searching for the tip of a nonexistent pipe to bite down on. And then answered in a pliant voice, "No, son, I guess you really don't." He turned and marched deeper into the woods. Larry scrambled behind him, making an argument of sorts, while doing his best to keep his footing in the wet, sloping snowdrifts.

Thomas Hardman did listen to his son's words, but he heard only his own thoughts. He had loved this island, he liked to tell people, since he opened his eyes. It hadn't been quite that long, his parents having first brought him to Burrows one month after his fifth birthday, only long enough to have been his whole life. Now his son wanted him to abandon it because age had tricked him and turned him old. This son who had abandoned the island while still a boy, how could he possibly understand a man who never left it.

For wanting you to live longer, his son had said. Those words stayed with Tom Hardman. How could he explain the difference between living and existing to this man?

"And what's gonna happen when one of you dies?" he heard Larry asking.

"We'll die," he shouted over his shoulder. "Don't see how we have much choice." No, that was unfair. This was supposed to be man talk, he remembered, and he was toying with a boy. Stopping again, he faced Larry. "When your mother or I die, son, then whoever is left'll have to decide what's the right thing to do. But that's not a decision you make early."

Larry kept his eyes buried in the snow as he followed his father. The walking was difficult because of the soft underfooting. Each step required him to push his toe firmly into the snow, test its firmness, and only after it had proved strong, let his whole weight down. When possible, he walked in the footsteps made by his father. The irony of that was not lost to him.

He would eventually win this war. Time, not logic, was his great weapon, and it would eventually leave his mother and father no choice but surrender. But he didn't want to wait till then, until the old man was forced to concede. He wanted his father to move now, to make that choice freely and to learn to enjoy the remaining years of his life.

Convincing him would be difficult, he knew that. The old man's too proud, he had explained to Diane, it'll take some time. So this was just his opening foray. A simple scouting expedition.

That made him press the battle. "Dad, I know you don't want to hear this, but your island is dying. It's forgotten and you and Mom are being forgotten right along with it. There's no life for you here anymore."

Thomas Hardman was listening to every word now.

"When was the last time you sat back and relaxed? What you have here isn't a life, it's a fight for survival. Diane and I want you to enjoy these years. See your grand-children grow up. You've earned the right."

Tom knew his son meant well.

"Leave this damn island and go with us."

Great anger rose inside Tom Hardman as he heard Larry blaspheme the island and so, without the moment of thought he had promised himself, he turned around on his son. "You forgot everything I taught you, didn't you? Your mind's got messed up by that city. It's gotten clogged up by that air you breathe, by people pushing and shoving you all the time. Well, that's not for me. I'd rather die here, thank you."

He didn't wait for an answer, but tramped on ahead, moving faster through the snow-covered woods than he had before.

They were twenty-five minutes deep into the forest when Tom stopped by the big evergreen and leaned down into the snow. At first Larry couldn't see what he was doing, then he saw a scramble of snow billowing into the air. Stepping closer, he saw light pink stains on the snow, then the thrashing rabbit, camouflaged against the white, snared in the lightweight steel trap. A trickle of blood seeped slowly from its torn leg.

Larry watched as his father tried to pry open the trap. "I thought you never trapped animals," he said, almost victoriously.

After working at the trap for a moment, Tom walked around the tree and reappeared with a thick, twisted branch. Holding the branch with two hands, he lifted it high into the air, then smashed it down on the rabbit. The thrashing in the snow ceased. "When you're hungry," he answered, cutting the dead rabbit loose with his pocket knife, "you do just what you have to do to survive." He had killed.

"There's more to life than just surviving, you know. If you—"

Tom did not want the argument to continue any longer. "Sometimes surviving is enough."

Larry bent down to help his father with the rabbit.

"Don't touch it!" Tom shouted at him. Then added, sarcastically, "I wouldn't want you to get blood all over your city clothes." He knew his son would never understand.

Inside the house, by the warmth of the living-room fire, Diane was similarly testing. Her purpose was not to persuade Frieda Hardman to come into the city, rather to test the firmness of the ground she stood on. "Will Larry be able to convince him?" she asked. They both knew what the question was.

Frieda was knitting a sweater that Josh would have to grow into. Without missing a stitch, she answered assuredly, "No."

Diane sat perched in the easy chair, a magazine on her lap, legs partially tucked under her body, and waited for her mother-in-law to elaborate. She did not, forcing Diane to ask, "Why?"

Frieda stopped her knitting. "Thomas Hardman brought me to this island forty-one years ago, and we've been here ever since. He doesn't see any reason to leave now."

"And you?"

She returned to her needles. "I'm his wife." And that is something, she thought, that you could never understand.

On their walk back to the house the two men heard the clamorous barking of the pack somewhere in the distance. "Just a bunch of abandoned dogs," Tom explained. "They're hungry."

"They're loud," Larry answered. "Are they dangerous?"

"They're just dogs," Tom told him, a slight edge of irritation in his voice.

In the house the children played with plastic blocks, building dream castles, Diane finished marking up the December issue of *Vogue,* and Frieda struggled to get the arms even on the bulky knit sweater.

The big shepherd led his pack to the western side of the gorge. Then the pack started moving along its rim, slowly passing each of the small, isolated, deserted island houses.

Searching.

THREE

Larry could not sleep that night. Although his legs ached from the long walk through the snow and his body was tired, his mind was so alive with thoughts he could do nothing but lie quietly on the bed, listening to his wife's deep breathing. The house was warmly quiet, content, and sometime in the night he got up from bed and walked to the window.

This bedroom had once been his. The walls had since been painted over, the bureau he had carved up with his official scout knife had been replaced, and the special boyish smell that always seemed to hang over the room was gone, but it was still, and would always be, his room. He ran his fingers over the cracking paint on the window sill, his mind seeking memories. Then he squatted down and peered out the window as he had as a child.

The bright, full moon outside made a sparkling path from the sky directly to his window, diamonds of fantasy gleaming off the snow. The big leaning tree on the edge of the wood seemed to have tilted just a few inches more, and Larry remembered the autumn night he had first studied the shadow it cast in the moonlight and become frightened, thinking it to be the shadow of a witch. That thought led to another, and still another, until the memories flooded in. The Christmas he fell asleep standing at this window, waiting for Santa Claus to please bring him the promised bicycle. The summer he had first chicken pox, then measles, and had been forced to lay alone in this darkened room and watch the summer pass him by. The day they buried Uncle Harry, Uncle Harry with a single silly little patch of hair in the front of an otherwise bald scalp, he had watched from the window as they carried his coffin to the car. More memories. Dad coming home in the evening. Deer playing in the yard. Kenny being brought home from the mainland hospital.

Something moved in the yard.

So many thoughts, faces racing in and out of his mind, voices, movement in the yard, children playing.

Again, it moved.

His memory shut down and thrust him into the reality of the night. He stared down at the yard. There was nothing there. Nothing moved. Movement in his mind? Branches blowing in the casual breeze? His eyes carefully explored the yard, from gorge to house. And still he saw nothing.

Finally he looked over to the edge of the woods, beyond the gorge, just above the line of the fence top. Only then did he see the two balls of green fire reflecting the moonlight.

Eyes that seemed to be looking directly at him. His heart started racing, and he strained to see what it was that came out of the forest, but the night shadows made it impossible. The breeze gently pushed the tree branches, shedding more light on the edge of the gorge. And another pair of eyes looked on the house. Then disappeared.

He could not move from the spot. This most horrible fantasy, this boyhood nightmare, was finally coming true. The things of the forest finally coming after him, searching for him.

The eyes began to move. They were coming toward the house.

He saw them plainly only when they crossed the wooden bridge. Two small animals. Dogs? He waited and watched. They moved into the yard, into the moonlight. Dogs. One larger than the other, it was impossible to tell the breed. Cautiously, they walked around the house, seemingly searching. Larry stood absolutely still at the window, transfixed by their presence.

They inspected the house. After examining the front, they moved to the side, near the porch, out of his line of vision. He bent slightly with their movements, trying to follow them, but they had disappeared. He lifted his head and stared out into the yard again.

Eight more dogs had come from the forest and stood across the bridge, staring at the house.

Time passed, Larry had lost the ability to determine how long, and then the two scouts reappeared from behind the house. They stood in the middle of the yard, looking at the other dogs, as though transmitting a message. The other dogs began walking alongside the gorge, away from the forest. They walked in a straight line, almost marching. Twelve in line, plus the two still in yard. Fourteen.

Their bodies cast black shadows in the moonlight. With

the exception of one dog who had to struggle to keep up, they all seemed to be about the same size. The shadows passed by the house, out of Larry's line of vision. And still, the first two dogs remained in the yard. Finally the smaller of the two rose and trotted across the bridge, following the long line.

The last dog in the yard seemed to be gray, but Larry could not tell if that was his true color or the reflection of the moon. The dog waited until the rest of the pack was well clear of the house, then raised its snout to the stars and loosed a long, chilling howl. The cry tore through Larry.

The dog finished, turned and looked one final time at the house, then left the yard to catch up with the pack.

Larry knelt frozen at the window, staring down into the yard, as if he expected the tracks that now circled the house suddenly to disappear. Gradually, he began to be aware of feeling in his body again. His mouth was parched. His already sore legs were aching. And a single drop of sweat meandered its way down the small of his back.

The night was crisp and perfectly clear. The shepherd sat in the yard, watching as the pack passed along the ridge. No food here, he had communicated, we must move on, beyond the protection of the forest. The pack could no longer sleep through the night. Death had touched it. The dogs would have to hunt until they found food.

Whatever food there was.

Larry was unusually quiet during the huge breakfast his mother prepared the next morning, his thoughts still on the dogs that had come in the night. He decided to say nothing to Diane or his mother—there was no need to worry them—but when he was alone with his father, he intended to find out more about this pack.

They worried him. More, he realized, than they should. They were just dogs, and dogs could be frightened away, ignored, or even shot if it came to that. Yet something about the pack was strange. The way the big dog in the yard seemed to command them. They way they marched so perfectly, so organized. And finally, he understood what it was that made him so uneasy. The dogs seemed to have a purpose.

The morning reflected the night before, crisp and clear. A morning to feel alive in. An island morning. Larry had forgotten how beautiful the island could be, one of the penalties he paid for living in the city. His father spent the morning doing small chores inside the house, so Larry didn't have a chance to speak to him. Twice during the morning he went to the kitchen window to check the yard. The prints were still there, but in the daylight they seemed less threatening.

The opportunity to question his father came early in the sunny afternoon, when they went out back together to chop wood. Larry took the long-handled ax and started biting into the woodpile. At first he said nothing, concentrating on matching each of his father's blows with one of his own. Only when Tom Hardman stopped to lean on his ax handle and catch his breath, did he ease into conversation. "Those dogs we heard yesterday," he began, as if asking his father if he remembered the howls, "I saw them in the yard last night."

Tom Hardman was not a big man physically, but he possessed great strength built from years of driving a sharpened metal wedge into hard wood. He said nothing as he lifted his ax once more and smashed down.

"I was wondering about them," Larry continued. "Where'd they come from? How long have they been here?"

Chop! Tom's ax crashed into the log. "They bother you?"

Larry didn't hesitate. "I guess they did. I guess they shook me up a little."

Chop! The dull thud boomed through the clear air. "Yeah. They been doing that to some other people on this island too. Some of 'em wanted to hunt them down." Chop! "I talked 'em out of it." He rested, leaning heavily on the curved wooden shaft. "Larry, they're just dogs. Maybe damn hungry dogs, but still just dogs."

"Are they dangerous?"

The same question. "No," he said, still convinced they were not. "See, son, these dogs are—" He never finished the sentence.

A desperate scream ripped through the air. Larry recognized it instantly: Diane's voice. From in front of the house. He dropped his ax and started running. Tom, still holding his ax, followed a step behind.

At first Larry did not understand exactly what was happening. All he saw was Diane, standing coatless in the center of the yard, her fist clenched tight against her mouth. Only when he followed her line of vision to the bridge did he see them. Five of them, the gray shepherd in front, sitting calmly on the other side of the gorge.

And walking toward them, clutching her doll close to her chest, was his daughter.

"Marcy!" he screamed sharply.

The child turned around and smiled at her father, then pointed to the five animals. "Dopey dogs," she explained innocently, as she walked on.

Diane started after her, but before she took two steps Larry grabbed her arm and held her. "Wait," he warned, "don't excite them."

Tom stood just behind them, and slightly to the right. Slowly, cautiously, making each move smooth and natural, he hoisted his ax and began walking toward the bridge. "Honey," he sang softly to Marcy, "come to Grampa."

"Dopey," she explained again, as if it were the most obvious thing in the world, then continued moving toward them.

The five dogs watched the girl closely. Through their color-blind eyes she appeared to be a mass of grays and blacks, lacking distinct edges, running together. They sensed the child more than they saw her, and somewhere inside these senses stirred memories of their pasts, of other children, and games, and warm houses, and food.

Marcy walked closer.

Inside the house Frieda stood silently over her sink, watching as she had watched her own children so many years before. Without even realizing it, she continued to wash and dry the breakfast dishes. Behind her, sleeping contentedly in front of the unlit fireplace with his arm draped around his dog, Josh was oblivious to the scene.

The shepherd rose and advanced to meet the child. As he did, from the corner of his eye, he saw one man moving toward him. Looking directly at Tom, he gave a short, sharp growl. This warning was understood. The man halted.

The shepherd met the child halfway between the bridge and the other dogs. He sniffed about her, recognizing immediately that this was not the child he once knew. Her smell was different. He pushed his big head hard against her arm, shoving her, demanding she rub him.

She pulled his ear. And laughed.

He jumped back, looked at her suspiciously, then stepped forward again. This time she scratched his head with her free hand.

Larry put his arm around Diane's shoulders and pulled her close. Her cold, fair skin was covered with small goosebumps. They stood motionless together. Watching.

Afraid even to breathe. Afraid to upset the delicate balance. Silent tears ran down Diane's face and dropped onto her blouse.

The shepherd moved back slightly and began to whine, remembering. He looked past the child, across the bridge, to the shapes standing in the front yard. They blended together in dark shades. Their smells ran together, sweet smells, but they were not odors he knew.

The smallest dog, the dachshund, stood up on its pudgy legs and started its strange waddle toward the shepherd and the child. The shepherd turned and glared, forcing the dachshund to stop in mid-waddle and lower its body to the ground.

Turning to the girl, the shepherd nuzzled her again. She tapped him on his snout and laughed. And tapped him a second time. The dog gave her a playful shove, pushing her backwards. "Nice doggy." She laughed, tapping him once more. The dog pushed her again, the shoves now becoming firmer, less playful.

Thomas Hardman mumbled something under his breath, too softly for either Larry or Diane to hear. His own private prayer.

Larry stood helplessly. Just dogs, he kept thinking, just dogs. There was nothing he could do to help his daughter. There was nothing he could do but stand in the cold and watch this big shepherd, bigger than she was, push and shove the child. Any move he made at the dogs might cause them to panic, and there was no figuring what they might do then. Better, he knew, to stand, and wait, and suffer. Helplessly.

The shepherd pushed Marcy again, and this time she almost tumbled backwards. Recovering her balance quickly, she managed to stay on her feet. Involuntarily, Diane strained forward. Larry tightened his grip on her arm, pushing deep red welts into her skin. "Bad doggy,"

Marcy scolded the shepherd, and hit him on the snout with her doll.

He bared his white teeth for the first time, and a low, fierce growl rose from deep in his throat. It was a threat, and a cry. Then he pushed her again, and only then, finally, Marcy understood what the dog wanted. Taking the doll from under her arm, she held it out for him to see. He sniffed it. Then took it in his mouth, holding it by the rubber arm and shook it violently. The doll's dress fluttered in the breeze, and crying sounds emerged from the middle of the toy, but the doll stayed intact.

The shepherd put it down in the snow and touched it lightly with his paws, pushing it along the ground. He did not really understand what it was, or where the cries it made came from. It had a different odor from the child. He licked it; it was not food. Yet there was something familiar about it, something he had known before.

He picked the doll up in his teeth and started walking back toward the other dogs, away from the child, away from the bridge.

"Dolly mine!" Marcy cried, starting after him.

A soft voice carried from the kitchen door. "Marcy," Frieda called, "come and have a cookie." The child hesitated, looked at the dog carrying her doll, looked back at her grandmother, stood indecisively for a few seconds, then started running happily toward the house. Diane tore loose from Larry's grip and ran to meet her. A few feet from the edge of the bridge she scooped her up into her arms and ran to the house, holding her cradled to her breast.

Tom and Larry watched as the dog carried the doll to the other animals. Each dog, in turn, sniffed it, touched it, licked it, pushed at it. Eventually the shepherd and the Labrador started pulling the doll open, tearing at it, ripping it, until simultaneously with a final artificial cry, its insides came bursting out.

54

"Get the gun," Larry told his father.

"Larry, I don't—"

"Get the gun," he ordered. His mouth was dry and tightly drawn, his eyes fixed on the dogs, as they pulled the remains of the doll apart.

The Winchester thirty-thirty hung over the living room fireplace. Thomas Hardman had little actual use for the rifle, but having its protection in the house had always made him feel more secure. He'd used it to teach Larry respect for weapons, and accuracy, and used it again to teach Kenny the same lessons. Twice each year, whether it had been fired or not, he took it down from its decorative perch and carefully oiled each piece.

The shells were hidden in a cardboard shoebox at the top of the bedroom closet, far beyond the reach of any child. In fact, Tom had to strain to reach them himself. After a short struggle to get the box down, he selected six steel-jacketed bullets and carried them out to Larry.

His son took the weapon and ammunition without a word, slid one bullet into the chamber and hefted the rifle to his shoulder. It had been at least ten years since he'd held the Winchester and he was surprised that he'd forgotten how heavy it was. He pushed the stock securely into his shoulder, adjusted it for comfort, and sighted down the long barrel on the gray shepherd, the leader.

There was nothing more for Thomas Hardman to say. He still refused to believe the dogs were dangerous, but understood his arguments would have no effect on his son. His only thought was, get it over with.

The shepherd moved to the right. Larry shifted his aim slightly to the left, until the dog's head was once again in the middle of the cross hairs. He waited, held his breath, then gently squeezed the trigger.

The bullet pulled just barely to the right, much more than Larry had allowed for, slid by the gray shepherd and smashed into the head of the smaller shepherd who stood beside him. The dog's head exploded, showering bits of blood, brain, skin and fur onto the other dogs. The headless body collapsed, and its last few involuntary heartbeats pushed a small stream of bright red blood out of a severed vein into the snow.

The crash of the rifle sent the other dogs scurrying into the forest. All but the shepherd. The gray dog stood, ears erect, tail high, staring at Larry, almost disbelievingly. Then he let out a desperate howl of betrayal.

For a few seconds Larry was incapable of firing again. Then he pushed another shell into the rifle, quickly took aim, and squeezed off another shot. Again, he missed. The shepherd stood, coldly immobile, staunch, impregnable. Finally he turned and defiantly trotted to the protection of the woods. Larry's final shot, which landed just a few feet behind him, did not cause him to break his gait.

Larry lowered the gun and watched the dog disappear into the forest. "Bastard," he cursed quietly. His stomach churned with excitement and, although he would never admit it, he felt great satisfaction. He had protected his brood, proven himself. An island thing.

His first shot had been accidentally perfect. The force of the bullet had almost completely severed the battered head from the body, then driven the body backward. It lay where it fell. From the front yard neither Larry nor Tom could see the pool of blood forming just above the dog's neck, where its head had been.

The gray shepherd stopped just a few yards into the trees and turned for one final look at the body of his mate. His gaze went from the dead shepherd up, across the gorge, to the hunter. He would gather his pack quickly and they would forage again. But differently this time. This time they would be free of their memories, released from their early obedience training, finally free to hunt every prey. The single, shattering bullet had severed all human bonds.

Larry poured a spoonful of hot gravy over his meat. The day had built him an appetite, and he was determinedly working through a fourth slice of roast. "You know," he said with his mouth stuffed half full, "I've never seen anything like the way that shepherd took that doll." He was still burning excess energy. "Think they'll come back?" he asked his father.

Diane cut in. "Please, Larry," she pleaded, "please don't talk about it." She hadn't changed clothes for dinner, something she always did.

"We have to talk about it," he informed her in his most knowing voice. "We have to find out what's going on."

Tom had no real answer. "Animals are unpredictable," he said, his head bowed over his plate. "It doesn't make any sense for them to come back."

"So?"

"Nobody said dogs got any sense."

Frieda tried to change the subject, mentioning something about the children being sound asleep. When no one followed her lead, she left the table and started to wash the dishes. Diane stayed at the table and watched her.

"Are you still against hunting them?" Larry asked. "Now, I mean."

They were sitting at opposite sides of the table, facing each other, but neither of them looked up as they spoke. "I'm not sure," Tom answered. "They didn't hurt her, you know."

"This time!"

"This time," Tom agreed, finally looking at his son. "But, Larry, these aren't wild dogs. They're abandoned pets. City dogs, mostly. I think the reason they didn't harm

57

her is because they know children. These dogs have lived with people, they're not hunting dogs."

"You think that makes a difference?"

"Yes, I do. They were raised to trust humans. To obey them. The harder we make it for them, the more difficult they're going to be to control, assuming some of them manage to survive the winter." He added pointedly, "Which I doubt."

"So you think I did the wrong thing today?"

Tom said nothing.

"Don't you?"

Tom pushed his dessert around in the small china bowl as he spoke. "I don't know. I don't think we'll ever know. It's done, so there's no use wondering about it." As the low-key argument continued, Diane did her best to shut out any thoughts of the island. Instead she concentrated on New York, making mental lists of things to be done as soon as they returned to the apartment. They would have a party, she decided, a big party, she would find some excuse for it. This argument, the dogs, the island, none of it interested her. It was something for the two men, father and son, to talk out, and they might have continued a good part of the evening if Frieda had not looked up from her dish drying and seen a blood-covered face pressed against the kitchen window.

"Oh, my God," she said in a voice no louder than a whisper, "oh, my dear God." A china platter slipped from her fear-frozen hands and smashed on the floor.

The face began slipping away, sliding down the window. A bloody hand reached up and searched for something to grasp, but found nothing, then slid away, leaving only a thin line of blood on the pane.

Diane looked up when the platter smashed. She saw the face just before it disappeared, falling eyes open in terror, and tried to scream, but there was only silence.

Larry and Tom saw the face an instant after Diane. "Jesus," was all Larry could say.

Tom reached the kitchen door first, tore it open and ran outside, Larry trailing a step behind. The body had collapsed directly under the window, and they reached it even before it had fully settled in the snow. Long dark hair, matted with blood, partially covered the face, so it took Frieda a few seconds to recognize her friend. "Cornelia?" she asked. "Cornelia?"

Cornelia Cornwall opened her eyes, a grimace on her face, her lips caked with dried blood. She managed to utter one word.

"Dogs," she said.

Larry and Tom half dragged, half carried her into the house. Frieda hurried in behind them, bolting the door. By the time she wet a clean cloth, her husband and son had managed to lay the blood-covered woman on the living room couch.

The blood flowed from two slashes, one on her forehead, the other high on her scalp. Tom did his best to stop the bleeding, which by then was little more than a trickle. Cornelia lay quietly on the couch, staring straight ahead, her eyes wide open with terror.

As he pressed the cloth against her cuts, Tom bent close. "Corny," he said in his soft, calm voice, "it's Tom. Tell me what happened. Where's Charlie?"

She looked at him blankly. "Dogs," she repeated.

"I know," Tom whispered, "I know, Corny. But you have to tell me, where is Charlie?"

She smiled. "Charlie? Coming from town." She stopped, and remembered. The strange smile faded, and her mind saw everything happening all over again. "But the dogs ... the dogs ..." Suddenly she bolted upright and grabbed Tom tightly around his neck. "Help Charlie. Please, Tom. Help him." Her voice rose. "Help Charlie."

And then she screamed. "Help him! Help him! They're hurting him! Oh, no, no! Stop it, please stop it!" She tore at invisible attackers with her hands.

Tom slipped his arms around her, pulling her close. "It's all right, it's okay, Corny, we're gonna help him now." The woman's body shook with sobs, until finally she leaned against him and began to cry.

At a glance from Tom, Frieda replaced him on the couch, and held Corny as tight as she could.

Rising from the couch with a tired sigh, Tom said anxiously to Larry, "We better get over there."

Larry nodded. "What do you think?"

"I don't want to," his father answered. For the second time that day the Winchester was pulled down from its hooks over the fireplace. The shoebox of shells had been left on the mantel and Tom stuffed a handful into his pocket.

"I better have a weapon," Larry said.

Tom gazed about the room, his eyes finally stopping on the long, steel-pointed fireplace poker. "Here," he said, picking it up, "take this."

The poker was almost a yard long and made of black steel. Near its tip a short, sharpened, gold-colored curved spike protruded. Larry swung the rod with his right hand, testing its balance. "It'll do."

Diane had retreated into a far corner. At the sight of Cornelia, the full horror of what might have happened that afternoon had overwhelmed her. But now she moved forward. "You're not going out there," she told Larry. It was an order.

Larry ignored her as he pulled his heavy ski parka on over a bulky sweater.

She unbent slightly. "Don't go over there, Larry. Call the police, call the other people on the island. You don't know what's outside."

Larry looked over to his father. "Let's go."

Diane moved between the two men and the kitchen door. "Please, Larry. We don't even live on this island."

His eyes bored through her.

"I won't let you go!"

"Get out of the way, Diane," he ordered firmly.

For just the smallest slice of time they stood seeing each other. The loves, the hates, the ordeals of ten years of marriage compressed into a few seconds. And instantly, both understood that their life together would never be precisely the same. He was reclaiming powers he had so lovingly ceded to her.

She moved out of his way.

"Keep the children upstairs. Make sure all the doors and windows are locked. If you can, get her"—Larry nodded his head at Cornelia—"get her upstairs and stay with her." He paused. "Do you understand what I'm telling you?"

"But what are you going—"

"Do you understand everything I said?" he repeated in an irritated voice.

She replied hesitantly. "Yes. I think so."

"Good. Then go do it." She started to move away. "And, Diane. . . ."

She had known he would stop her. She had absolutely known it. Now he would apologize. "This time don't let the kids out of your sight for a minute."

There was no way to answer him.

Tom stood behind his son, listening to him reel off orders. There was nothing to be added, he decided, Larry had covered everything. Temporarily, he shut his great concern for the safety of his friend out of his mind, feeling nothing but pride. Pure fatherly pride in his son. On this day, this hour, he had enjoyed the rare privilege of watching his son finally take control of his life.

Now, he thought, now, when we have some time, we

61

can sit and talk about New York City. Man to man. Families should be together, and maybe it wasn't the worst place in the world to live.

Diane disappeared upstairs to check the children. Larry didn't share his father's confidence. What had been won, he knew, was the first skirmish. Diane was too tough an opponent to surrender meekly. She would wind her way through the battlefield of fashionable boutiques and private schools and sleek parties until the war could only turn her way. And then, only then, if he still wanted this fight, they just might destroy each other.

Tom looked across the long room at his wife. She was busy ministering to Corny and did not look up as her men left the house.

The night was dark and rapidly becoming colder. Clouds, the harbinger of a bad weather front moving off the Atlantic, had smothered the moon and the stars. Tom took his place in front, carrying the loaded rifle at his hip, with his son following five yards behind. They crossed the bridge and walked to the right, passing the '61 Chevy, which lay partially buried in a mound of snow. "The car?" Larry asked.

Tom shook his head and shouted over his shoulder, "Quicker to walk. Besides, it's too noisy. We want to be able to hear." They trudged on, setting out across the open field to the Cornwall house. It was quicker on foot, and gave them a clear view of anything approaching them.

Larry listened intently as their boots crunched rhythmically into the snow. He watched his breath steaming from his mouth, quickly disappearing before him. And he felt good. Not really frightened. Alive and exhilarated by this bizarre adventure. He could feel his heart pumping rapidly. This is what life is all about, he thought. No, he stopped and rephrased the thought, this is what I want my life to be about. Clean air, fresh water, open fields, this island. He remembered the first night in his life he had spent outdoors, an October camping trip with his father. They had set up a small tent in the woods, but slept outside, and he had counted stars until finally falling asleep. They had not been more than a thousand yards from the house, yet they were so alone they could have been civilization's last survivors.

That fall night, lying in the woods with his father, he had experienced total freedom for the first time. And now, as they tramped across the snow-covered open fields, he felt it once again. It had been a long time.

Tom marched straight ahead, oblivious to his son's mental wanderings, his mind speculating on the fate of Charlie Cornwall. What had happened? Why had the dogs attacked? And where were they now? He listened for them, but the only sound he heard was the wind swirling across the open field, and the crunch of their boots in the snow. Nothing moved as far as he could see, but he lifted the barrel of the Winchester a few inches and slid his index finger into the trigger housing. Just in case.

They walked straight for the house, two lone figures crossing a field of virgin snow. They saw the house for the first time when they reached the small knoll that overlooked it from a distance of a hundred yards. One light burned dimly in the kitchen, and there seemed to be a second light on in one of the upstairs rooms. From their distance the house looked perfectly calm. They started down the hill.

They stopped. A gust of wind blew the kitchen door open, and it slowly swung back and forth on creaking hinges. The house had been left open. No sound, no hint of movement, came from within. "Ready?" Tom asked uncomfortably.

"Yeah," Larry answered in a dry voice. He cleared his throat and started walking carefully toward the house. On the way down he discovered the first paw prints.

FOUR

Something vile had happened at this pretty little house. Something.

The front yard was covered with animal tracks. The snow in front of the house had been churned up, down to the brown earth in places, and there was a large stained area. In the dim, refracted light coming from inside it was impossible to determine precisely what color the stain was, and neither man would permit his mind to admit what he guessed. A single set of wide, human footprints, coming from the right, from the dirt road, led into the patch of stained snow. A smoother path, as if a heavy weight had been pulled over the snow, moved from the patch out toward the fields behind the Cornwall house. There were stains on the path, as well, and numerous tracks beside it.

Tom and Larry approached the house cautiously, avoiding the dirtied snow, never taking their eyes from the slowly swinging door. They said nothing to each other, but their minds worked together. Tom went directly to the door, while Larry turned his back to the house and began carefully surveying the surrounding area.

Thomas Hardman would not let himself imagine what horror might be waiting for him inside. Taking a deep breath, he shifted his grip on the rifle and shoved the kitchen door open with his foot.

There was no movement inside. He stood nervously in the doorway, letting his eyes adjust to the light, then silently entered the house.

"Charlie?" He knew there would be no answer. "Charlie, you here?" But he had to try. The house seemed untouched, everything in its proper place. He moved warily through the kitchen and into the living room.

He yelled again. "Charlie?" The wind answered him by blowing a newspaper off the low coffee table onto the worn area rug. There was no other sound. He paused after each step, and listened. Slowly, cautiously, Tom moved across the lower floor of the house toward the staircase.

The first step creaked badly when he put his weight on it, causing him to pause even longer than usual before trying the second step. The light upstairs seemed to be coming from the rear of the house.

He was on the seventh step when he heard the kitchen door slam behind him.

He froze, as beads of sweat broke out on his forehead. Without breathing, he turned his head toward the door. It suddenly burst open.

Larry moved instinctively when the door slammed. In one swift motion he reached the door and kicked it open, holding the poker high above his head, ready to sweep down with it. But the house was silent. "Dad?" he called.

Thomas Hardman breathed again. "Here," he answered.

Larry walked into the living room. "It was the wind, that's all." Looking around the cold, empty room, he asked, "You find anything?"

Tom had trouble catching his breath. "No. Not really. I was just going to look upstairs."

"Want me to do it?"

He did not. Charlie Cornwall was his closest friend. Whatever had happened to him, he knew, he had been responsible for. He had talked them out of hunting down the dogs; he had persuaded them to wait. Whatever was upstairs was private, between him and Charlie.

"I'll stay here," Larry said.

The stairs creaked all the way to the top. There were two bedrooms and one bathroom on the second floor.

The bathroom door and one bedroom door were closed. Trying to move silently, but unable to prevent the aged boards from moaning under his weight, Tom eased down the hallway, pausing at the first bedroom, which was open and lighted. Charlie's pajamas were laid out neatly on the bed.

He crossed the hallway to the bathroom. Silently, he gripped the doorknob and leaned against the door, listening. To silence. Then he twisted the knob and threw the door open. The room was black, but something light hunched in the corner, backed against the bathtub. Somehow Tom managed to find the light switch as he nimbly lifted the rifle and aimed. A baby blue towel lay piled on the floor. Outside the second bedroom, Tom hesitated briefly then flung open the door. As he knew it would be, the room was empty. The tension drained from him, the rifle barrel dipped, and he returned downstairs. When he saw his son he shook his head sadly.

"He's still outside then," Larry said matter-of-factly.

"I guess," Tom answered hollowly. "Let's follow the path." It seemed to be the only choice, but one which made no sense to Larry. He was sure they wouldn't be able to find anything in the night, and there didn't seem to be any compelling reason to risk stumbling around. Whatever had happened to Charlie Cornwall was over with. Finished. And they still did not know what was out there. Waiting.

He opened his mouth to explain these obvious facts to his father, then stopped. Tom had picked up a pair of silver-framed reading glasses from the table next to an overstuffed easy chair and was examining them closely. He let his fingers run around the frame, feeling the presence of their owner in the thin metal. Then he laid them down carefully, exactly as he found them. And Larry understood there was every reason to follow the path.

On the way out Tom picked up the telephone and dialed Ned Curtis' number. After letting it ring ten times he hung up, and moved to the door.

As they left the house, Larry checked the neck button on his parka to make sure it was clasped. "Who'd you call?" he asked. The cold was beginning to seep inside.

"Ned Stewart," Tom replied sullenly. Then he gave the house a final look, switched off the kitchen light and slammed the door. "I'll lead," he said.

They walked beside the path in the snow, searching for clues to the fate of Charlie Cornwall. They had gone about two hundred yards when they found a small rectangular piece of cloth half-buried in the snow. Tom held it up for inspection. It was a square of stained flannel material, and this time there could be no mistaking the stain. The fabric was covered with blood.

"Maybe we should go back now," Larry suggested softly.

Tom folded the wet cloth into fours and stuck it into his jacket pocket. Without answering his son, he walked on. Larry stood watching him, letting him take the lead, then checked the area behind them and started trailing.

The house disappeared behind a small rise. Larry's legs were beginning to feel the strain from pushing through the snow. The cold was part of him now, gnawing at him. The little toe on his left foot began throbbing. But still he crunched forward, fifteen yards behind his father, glancing left and right, then turning to check the rear. Step, he thought, step, step, step. He fell into cadence; one: one, two, three. He was so engrossed in counting, walking, trying to ignore the cold, living to conserve his dwindling reservoir of energy that he almost crashed into his father.

Tom had stopped along the edge of the path and was staring into the snow.

"What is it?" Larry asked.

Tom answered by pointing down with the Winchester barrel. Larry followed the barrel into the snow and, at first, could not determine exactly what he was looking at. It was a twisted strip about seven inches long and an inch wide, dark against the light snow. Only after a few seconds did the edges take form in his mind and he realized he was staring at a slice of human scalp. Most of it was covered with curly gray and white hair, but the bald portions of skin had already turned black.

At first he found it impossible to avert his eyes. Then he felt his insides swelling and he threw up.

Tom did not move. He stood riveted, his eyes locked to that flesh and all the horrors it represented.

Reaching down, Larry picked up a handful of fresh snow and thrust it into his mouth, trying to wash away the putrid taste of vomit. The taste gradually disappeared, but the searing pain in his stomach remained. He managed to catch his breath, but he simply could not bring himself to look at the slice of scalp again. Instinct crowded out reality, and he knew they had to get out of the field, had to get back to the safety of home. "Let's go now, Dad," he urged desperately.

Tom did not seem to hear him, so Larry took hold of his father's jacket, tugged slightly, and repeated the words. The old man turned toward him then and said in a distant voice, "Leave me alone, son."

Larry spoke again, more forcefully this time. "Dad, we've got to get home."

Thomas Hardman looked at his son, who he knew could never understand the feelings that were tearing at him. "Don't you see, son," he continued, half choking, "this is all my fault. I did this." His voice rose as he shut his eyes and confessed, "I did this!"

And then he was calm.

He opened his eyes to look helplessly at Larry. His

lower lip quivered as a tear wound its way down his face. "I did this," he said in a broken voice, "I'm so sorry."

And then the old man cried.

Larry took the Winchester from him and watched the fields as the old man released his grief. He waited until his father tried to hold back the tears, then said forcefully, "We have to get home now. Understand?"

Tom wiped his eyes. "I'm okay."

He was not, Larry knew, he was on the verge of shock, but they had to start moving. The dogs were out there. Somewhere. At first they walked together, then Larry took a ten-foot lead, turning every few steps to make sure his father was keeping up. The old man was buried in a flurry of thoughts, barely maintaining the pace.

Larry cut across the field, moving diagonally through the path, homing in on the ridge above the Cornwall house. When they reached it, he briefly considered stopping to telephone for help, but rejected that in favor of getting him home. Besides, he doubted his father could take the strain of sitting in Charlie Cornwall's house. Not after that.

Larry counted steps, trying to keep his mind clear. He constantly checked his father, slowing down when he dropped back, waiting for him to catch up.

Tom felt nothing of the night. His mind held only Charlie Cornwall's voice. "If anything should happen, you're gonna be the man we look to." Now it had happened. Who would be next? He had been wrong, and so his best friend was dead. The dogs would have to die now, he would have to hunt them down and kill them. He understood that. But that would not relieve the massive guilt he carried. The cold did not bother him at all.

Larry hummed bits and pieces of popular songs he remembered. He refused to think about the cold, or the fate of Charlie Cornwall. Getting home was all that mattered now, getting home to safety. Larry figured they were almost exactly halfway between the Cornwall house and home when they first heard the chilling chorus of howls.

Diane had done exactly as her husband ordered. The children were asleep in their upstairs bedroom. With Frieda's help she'd managed to get Cornelia upstairs and into the second bedroom. All the windows and doors were locked, and there seemed nothing left to do. So she took the small bottle of Ultra Lucent Caramel Frost from her cosmetic case and, as she listened to Frieda try to console Corny, carefully did her nails.

Cornelia's incoherent ramblings made no sense at all to her. Nothing seemed to connect. Charlie at the store. Charlie in his car. Dogs. An anniversary of some event. No grandchildren. Dogs at the front door. Charlie in his car. Once, in the middle of a memory, Corny's mind relived the terror. She sat up on the bed and screamed.

Diane left the room then. She checked on Josh and Marcy, who stirred but did not wake, and then stood at the window at the end of the upstairs hall, watching for her husband. The yard was beautiful in its white cover. The trees on the edge of the forest were topped with snowcapped branches. A reflection from the kitchen light swept over the area, casting long shadows. Diane stood looking at the winter scene, casually waving her wet nails in the air to dry, but this time its beauty eluded her. She wanted her husband back.

She had calmed considerably, and although her stomach churned with anxiety, outwardly she seemed at ease. He's always been able to take care of himself, she thought. But that was in a city world. The world he knew. On the isle of Manhattan he was a huntsman. Here, almost a stranger. How much could he know about wild dogs? Or surviving outdoors? Until this afternoon she hadn't even known he could handle a gun. She leaned against the windowsill and waited, thinking about the ragged, ugly dogs that had come out of the forest. Savage, filthy vicious beasts. But killers? Was it possible?

Diane had been standing there only a few minutes when she felt the touch of animal fur on her leg. She was barely able to stifle a scream as Dopey thrust against her leg. She leaned down to pat him, more nervous now than moments before.

The dogs were still a good distance away, but they were rapidly drawing closer. It was impossible to tell exactly how far away they were. But they certainly were moving toward them. Larry quickened the pace.

Larry couldn't be sure the pack sensed their presence. Dogs' eyesight, he knew, was not that good and surely they were too far away to use their excellent sense of smell. His logical mind told him it would be difficult, maybe impossible, for the dogs to find them at that distance. Yet, somehow, he knew. The dogs were coming for them. He broke into an easy lope, lifting his legs high in and out of the snow. His father struggled to keep up as best he could.

The gray shepherd led his pack across the fields. A few moments earlier the dogs had been resting peacefully, satiated. They had killed and fed. Then the oversized olfactory receptor area in the German shepherd's brain had been activated, and his nose, perhaps a million times more sensitive than that of man, had picked a familiar scent off the wind. It had been examined briefly, found acceptable, and transmitted to that part of his brain that translated scent to message. The message it carried was simple: The enemy was at large. The shepherd was incapable of remembering the man shooting its mate, but instead felt the deep pain caused by this scent. His mind could not make all the jumps that would lead to revenge, but the dog knew absolutely that this was the enemy and this enemy must die. So, honing on this unmistakable, constantly moving scent, the dogs closed in on Thomas and Larry Hardman.

Diane returned to the bedroom to sit with the two older women. Corny was quiet now, half asleep. Somewhere, in the distance, Diane thought she heard the baying of dogs. An overactive imagination, she decided, but an involuntary shiver ran through her body.

Despite the cold, Larry was beginning to sweat as he ran through the snow. Tom was unable to maintain the pace and fell gradually farther and farther behind. The dogs were nearer now, their sound a clatter of yelps. Larry no longer doubted their target, but somehow he did not feel afraid. Instead, inexplicably, he felt the exhilaration of cutting through the clear, crisp night, confident, in control, a perfectly operating machine, immune from danger.

The dogs' cries first pierced Tom's consciousness when he was about a quarter of a mile from the house. Initially the howls terrified him, and he attempted to run faster. But then complicated thoughts took control of his body, and he slowed to a jog, then stopped completely. It was time to meet and kill these animals. He turned toward the baying pack and waited. Glancing down into the snow, he imagined he saw Charlie's torn body at his feet. Now he would meet this pack of wild dogs, these barbarous animals that maimed and killed. And he would destroy them. It was that simple.

Larry, at the top of the rise, spotted the brightly lit house. They had made it. They were safe. The dogs would not catch them, and tomorrow, in the daylight, they would hunt down the pack and destroy it. He looked over his shoulder, expecting to see his father. Instead he saw him standing defiantly in the snow, watching the approach of the dogs. A flicker of fear ran through him. "Dad," he shouted into the wind, "Dad!"

Tom looked up at his son and gave a brief wave. Don't worry, the gesture said, I'll kill them for you.

The dogs emerged from a slight depression in the field and swept toward them, a furious juggernaut gliding on a white sea.

As soon as he realized his father's intention Larry started scrambling back toward him, calling, pleading, kicking up clouds of snow in his haste. Thomas Hardman did not hear him. His hatred for the dogs shut everything else from his mind.

The pack moved evenly, gracefully. Several of the dogs seemed to disappear in the snow with each bound, suddenly reappearing as they leaped forward. The last dog was the dachshund, who had great trouble running in the snow. The shepherd led. Mouth open, ivory teeth gleaming, ears laid back, the gray leader maneuvered his swarm directly toward his victims.

Thomas Hardman lifted his poker high into the air and waited. Without bothering to aim, Larry fired the Winchester. The bullet buried itself harmlessly in the snow sending up a spray of snowflakes. Undeterred, the dogs kept coming, straight at Thomas Hardman.

Three of them leaped at him as one. Whipping the poker through the air, he smashed it into the head of a large greyhound and felt the dog's skull crush beneath his blow. For his friend. And even when the combined weight of the two other dogs sent him sprawling into the snow he was content, still trying to swing his metal club.

Larry stumbled, tripped, fell face forward into the snow, then recovered, pushing himself toward his father. Thomas Hardman had disappeared under a flurry of snow kicked up by the struggling dogs, and all Larry could see were yelping, growling dogs fighting each other for position. He could not even hear his father's screams.

But before he could reach the swirl of bodies, the shepherd came at him.

Lifting the rifle to his hip, Larry aimed at the closing dog and pulled the trigger. The gun clicked, but failed to fire. He pulled the trigger again. Then the shepherd was on him, a seventy-four-pound missile. Grabbing the barrel of the Winchester, Larry tried to swing the gun as a club. The closeness of the dog prevented him from putting any real strength behind his blow, but the gun caught the dog in its side, smashing into its ribs, and sending it careening to one side.

Pain tore through the shepherd, howling giving way to yelps as it smashed into the ground, momentarily stunned. Larry ran to his father, now completely buried under the pack.

He swung the rifle again and again, smashing at the dogs. Blood spattered to mix with the snow. The dogs seemed to hesitate for a moment, then several broke away. Larry saw his father. One side of Thomas Hardman's face had been sliced open and blood poured from a gaping wound. Larry reached down, and as he did a scraggly collie hit him full force from the side, knocking him to one knee. The gold and white dog tried to dig its sharp teeth into the skin above Larry's left eye, but somehow he managed to push the steel barrel of the Winchester against the dog's throat. Abruptly he thrust a leg out, kicking the dog hard in the stomach, then smashed the rifle across the dog's back with such force that the gun snapped in half, its barrel flying off to one side.

The barrel was useless as a weapon. Desperately, he looked around, but there were no weapons in the snow. His father was still down, the dogs swarming over him. Larry heard the terrible sound of flesh being torn from

74

bone, heard his father scream. Tom continued to struggle for a few seconds, but then his body went limp.

Larry could not tell exactly when he died.

Terror-stricken, he fled, turning and running for the house. He reached the bridge. Behind him he heard two or three dogs closing in on him. He had seen the dogs, he had witnessed their terrible ability to destroy and he knew he was running for his life.

The single shot Larry managed to get off reverberated through the house. But even before the women could comprehend its meaning, the cry of the pack broke the silence. The barrage of howls and barks caused Corny to remember, and once again she became hysterical. Frieda did her best to comfort her, as Diane rushed to the window to see what was happening.

At first there was nothing visible in the blackness. Then she saw movement in the distance, although it was too dark to determine exactly what it was. She counted the seconds, listening to the sounds, her vigil paying off as she saw a figure race across the bridge. Even before she could turn to go downstairs, three dogs streaked into sight. She ran to the kitchen.

Larry smashed against the locked front door, the dogs right behind him. Knowing instinctively it was his only chance, he ran to the kitchen window, balled his hand into a fist and smashed it through the glass. Quickly he reached inside the broken window to open the hook lock. With a grunt he lifted the window, starting to climb inside even as he did.

His head was bent low as he fell over the sink and onto the kitchen floor. It wasn't until he had regained his feet that he saw Diane standing helplessly on the other side of the room.

Four steps away from the locked door.

Four steps away from helping him.

Blood flowed from his hand, spattering onto the tile in neat globules, and he became aware he had cut himself on window glass. But there seemed to be nothing for him to say.

Diane tried to speak, but couldn't. She stood frozen in the entrance to the kitchen as the first dog leaped through the open window.

FIVE

A tan Airedale bitch was the first dog to enter the house. She landed on the edge of the sink, slipping slightly on the Formica, then sprang through the air at Larry.

He punched at her, catching her on the side of the muzzle, sending her sprawling awkwardly across the linoleum floor. But before he could recover, two more dogs, a black boxer and a brown-and-white dalmatian, leaped through the window and at him. Larry fought back, punching and kicking, somehow managing to keep them away.

"Close the window," he screamed at Diane. "Close the goddamn window!"

She pushed herself back against the counter, trying to will her body to move, unable to make it respond to her commands. Petrified, she watched.

Larry's eyes bulged and thick veins stood out on his forehead. Gradually, the dogs forced him back against the sink.

Upstairs, Josh awoke and crawled out of bed. He had been taught how to open locked doors, and thus had no difficulty twisting the aged lock. Leaving his sister alone, he started downstairs.

The battered Airedale caught Larry's parka in her ivory teeth, but couldn't hold on. As she fell back, she ripped the jacket open. Immediately she leaped again, higher this time, snapping furiously at Larry's face.

As Frieda listened to the battle raging beneath her, she held Corny's head to her breast. And prayed.

The boxer and dalmatian helped press the attack, but by wedging Larry into the corner where the sink joined the counter the dogs had made it difficult for more than one of them at a time to get at him.

Frantically, Larry thrust his hand into the soap-filled sink, searching for a weapon. His fingers suddenly felt the blade of a carving knife. As the Airedale launched another leap, he grasped the knife and lunged at her.

The knife dug deep into the dog's guts, and an explosion of blood burst from the wound. The knife snapped as the Airedale's momentum carried her forward. She landed flat on her side, the blade embedded in her stomach. She lay there, panting softly, as her life ebbed out on the linoleum floor.

The other dogs backed off sensing the battle had turned, and leaped onto the sink, then out the window.

Josh walked into the kitchen, almost slipping on the thin sheet of blood spreading across the floor. He looked around, unable to understand what had happened, and ran to his mother, throwing his arms around her legs.

Finally Diane responded. She clasped her son tightly as the choking sobs began.

Larry was not aware of Diane's weeping. His brain refused to accept new information as it worked to clear the shocks of the past minutes. His clothes were speckled with blood, his father's, the dog's, and the droplets oozing from his wounded hand. He closed his eyes and slid down the counter to a sitting position, his head drooping between his legs.

It was summer in Central Park. He was on the Sheep Meadow with Josh and Marcy flying a silver kite with a long Mylar tail. The wind swept it high above all the other kites, until it was just a silent speck against the blue sky. Dopey was playing at his feet, rolling in the dirt-grass with the children jumping happily. And the sun beat down on them all, the hot summer sun warming them. "Higher, Daddy," Marcy squealed joyfully, "make it go higher."

"Larry?" The voice was far away. He did not recognize it. "Larry?" It pleaded for his attention. "Please wake up." He saw the five letters of his name floating through a black void. They were blue, edged in white, and they flashed on and off as they floated by. "Larry. Larry, please. Please wake up." He opened his eyes without actually planning to, and light filtered in. Too much light, too quickly, he had to shut them again.

"Open your eyes, Larry."

He opened them a second time. A woman was there, close to him. Her breath was warm on his cold face. She had a round face, but her eyes were puffy. Diane. His wife. The connections were difficult to make. "Larry?" Now he understood. It was her voice calling him.

He managed to open his eyes a bit wider. What did she want? "Larry?" Each breath burned. His throat, seared by the cold, flamed with each intake of air. His hand and side hurt. Sharp, burning pain in his hand, a dull, heavy throbbing sensation in his side.

Diane was wiping his face with a wet cloth. Nice. His legs, bent at the knees, ached. He managed to straighten them on the bloody floor. But why was he sitting there?

His mind was blank. The events had not happened, Time had ceased to exist. "What happened?" he asked Diane.

"Oh, Larry," she managed before another rush of tears cut off her voice. He tried to remember. Last night, he

remembered last night. The dogs! They had frightened him. He shivered. Then, he was concentrating now, he remembered the afternoon. Marcy had been playing in the yard and ... and the dogs. Dogs? The pack. He saw them clearly. He had blown one of them apart with the Winchester. In his mind he again saw the shepherd's head explode, this time in slow motion, thousands of bits of flesh and brain scattering through the air. But then....
Then.... What had happened? Something important. But he could not remember.

The surf washed over him and the wet beach. He rolled over in its coolness and pushed his nude body against hers. His right hand touched her thigh and swept upward until it cupped her breast. Her body was quite beautiful, breasts that stood high and firm, even as she lay on her back, bronze skin that ran tightly around swelling curves, and long, perfectly shaped legs that seemed made to fit around his body. Droplets of water had caught in her body hair and hung there, reflecting the moonlight of the Hawaiian evening. Now he slid his hand down the valleys of her body until he could gently rub the inside of her thigh. She arched in pleasure, and his hand ran up her body until he found the heart of her sex. She smiled. He eased up onto his left elbow, placing his lips on hers. His tongue ran deep into her mouth, probing, and she drew him closer. Her tan legs entangled his body, tightening around him until they were one, and he felt the warmth inside her.

A dog barked. Instantly he saw his father's torn, blood-covered face. It all came racing back as he remembered. The dogs, the fight in the snow, his father buried under the raging pack. And Charlie Cornwall's bloody scalp in the snow. He remembered each detail. And the weight of those memories exhausted him. "I'm okay," he said in an almost inaudible voice, "I'm all right now."

Dopey Dog had followed Josh into the room, his bark

jolting Larry's memory. The smells that filled the kitchen excited the dog. He sniffed at the carcass of the dead Airedale and a half whine, half growl rose from his throat. "Stop that, you silly Dopey!" Josh ordered and slapped the dog on its nose. Dopey whimpered and ran from the room.

The throbbing pain in his side seemed to be subsiding, and using the counter as support, Larry managed to stand up.

Diane was looking at him expectantly, seemingly waiting for him to say something. Their eyes met, but there was nothing for him to say. His mouth was parched and burning, filled with the taste of vomit. Leaning against the sink for support, he ran the cold water and stuck his head underneath the tap. The cold startled him back to complete consciousness. He filled his mouth with water, swallowed it, then relaxed as it flowed deliciously down into his stomach. Dripping but refreshed, he turned to face his wife.

She had not taken her eyes from him. "The dogs," he sighed, discovering his rib cage hurt when he spoke. He had great trouble going on.

"The dogs," he explained. But what were the right words to use? How could he explain what had happened out there? His left hand wandered aimlessly through the air as if trying to seize the right words.

"My father...." No, that was not right. "They ..." and only then did he understand there were no words to explain this horror. "The dogs," he said with finality. "The pack."

Frieda Hardman stepped into the kitchen and her son's eyes told her. Her face tightened in pain, and she slumped into a kitchen chair. For a moment she was silent, thinking, and then she folded her arms and cried into them.

Summoning the remainder of his strength, Larry lifted

her from the chair and led her into the living room. "Do we have anything to give her?" Larry demanded of his wife in a tired voice.

"I don't know," Diane hesitated, fumbling for a helpful answer. "I have some pills. You know, my Valium."

Her tranquilizers. Her little colored dailies, she called them. Pills for dieting. Pills for sleeping. Pills to speed her up; pills to slow her down. Her pills to get through the day. "Get them," he ordered, his voice beginning to recover some of its timbre. Frieda swallowed the pills easily, and gradually her crying gave way to deep breathing. With Diane's help, Larry managed to get her upstairs and into bed. Almost instantly she fell off to sleep. Only then did Larry change his wet, bloody clothes.

The cold air blowing through the smashed window-pane, the blood-soiled linoleum tiles and the carcass of the Airedale served as reminders of the battle that had taken place in the kitchen. The window would have to be taken care of first, and he began looking for something to use to cover the broken pane. Diane followed close behind, as if afraid to stray from his side, Josh holding tightly to her pants leg.

"Daddy," the boy began, "how do you—"

"Get him out of here," Larry directed his wife. "I don't want him here."

Diane took the child by his hand and was almost to the door when she halted. "He wouldn't be," she blurted, "if you hadn't dragged us here to start with!"

Larry shut his eyes. This was not a time to fight with her. Not now, not here. "Diane," he cautioned.

The tension of the night burst from her in a torrent of accusations. "It was you, Larry! You made us come here. I didn't want to. You forced me to bring my children to this . . . this place for your own selfish reasons. You didn't care about us. All you cared about was your precious. . . ."

Her voice rose as Larry waited impassively for her to finish her tirade. "I hate you!" she shrieked. "I hate you! Hate you!" She ran at him, beating her clenched fists against his chest. He let her work out her frustration, but when she began to cry, he caught her wrists tightly. At last, when he could take no more, he released her left wrist and smacked her solidly across the face with his open right hand.

The crack of the blow resounded through the room. He let go of her wrist, but her arm remained suspended. It hung in midair. She glared at him, said nothing, then strode quickly from the room, trailed by a wide-eyed Josh.

Left alone, Larry could feel his heart pounding wildly. He washed his wounded hand as best he could, examining the cut for slivers of glass. When he was satisfied the wound was clean, he wrapped his hand in a towel and sat down at the kitchen table.

The past forty-five minutes had been an eternity. He knew it couldn't be more than nine o'clock, but it seemed days had passed since the shooting in the front yard. Everything had happened so fast. He had had no time to do anything but react without thinking. Pure animal instinct. Even now his mind would not go beyond the simple facts. The dogs had become killers. Something had turned these pets—pets, he laughed at the word—something had turned them into beasts. Cornwall was dead. His father was dead.

Thomas Hardman, flinty old Thomas Hardman, dead? That sweet, gentle man? It didn't seem at all reasonable. Larry recalled the fight and began to search his conscience. Could he have saved him? Was there something he could have done to help him? What? He had run. He tried to remember what had been on his mind when he ran. Panic, he decided. But had he known his father was dead when he ran? Had he really known? Yes, he told himself, yes, yes,

yes. The old man had been dead. That stubborn old man had been dead.

Yet he knew there was no way he could be sure. He saw himself running again. He felt the cold air burning his lungs. His father had stopped on the path to wait for the pack. Run! The old man had wanted to die, blaming himself for Charlie's death. Could he have saved his father's life? Had he panicked? Was the old man dead? Larry realized he would never know.

He tried to push the past from his mind. "It's done," he said aloud. What he had to do now was get his family, his mother, and Corny off the island as quickly as possible. He needed a plan. But in his mind he was still running, taking long, leaping strides toward safety. The picture would not fade away. Get off the island, that was the important thing. In the morning everyone would crowd into the car and they would drive to town. He would summon an emergency boat over.... But he ran! It had been the only way. The only possible way. The old man stood there. He just *stood* there! Thomas Hardman had been dead when he ran.... Back to the city, try to work out some sort of accommodation with Diane. They couldn't go back to the way they lived before, he knew that, but they were intelligent, reasonable people, and they had the two children to consider. Maybe he shouldn't have hit her. Maybe he shouldn't have run.

He twisted his hands in anguish. The towel fell to the floor and he noticed that there were still blood stains embedded in his hand. His father's blood? A dog's blood? His own? No matter. What mattered was his father's death—and getting off the island. His mind was preoccupied with the past and future, so it was several minutes before he heard the baying of the pack.

He stiffened. They were back. Slowly, he moved to the broken window. The breeze was cold on his wet hair.

Outside, in a semicircle in the snow, sat the pack. These murderous animals had returned. They were not yet done with their killing. He laughed involuntarily.

The gray shepherd lifted his muzzle to the sky and a long keening filled the air, a cry of triumph, a warning and a voice of despair. His pack had fed. It had killed and eaten and now it would survive. The last bonds with domestic life had been broken. No memories of households, of human owners, remained. The pack had survived and would continue to survive. The shepherd bayed once more, a mournful sound that ricocheted through the house.

Larry watched unbelievingly. His eyes told him the obvious, a pack of dogs were sitting in the yard. But these things weren't dogs. Dogs were pets, docile animals that lived in the house, slept on the bed, came when called, fetched the newspaper, and rolled over on command. They had no minds of their own, they didn't think or question or entertain ideas. They were led and they followed.

He had owned dogs growing up on the island. One, a hound called Plato, had jumped into the lake when he thought Larry was drowning, risking his life to save Larry's. But even Plato was just a long-eared dog. A faithful, loyal, loving pet. Man's best friend.

But these animals in the front yard, these aberrations, what were they? Seeing them lolling in the snow, Larry found it impossible to believe what he knew to be true. They seemed so peaceful. A big Labrador retriever walked a tight circle before settling down comfortably. A handsome dog. Once some human's faithful companion. That had learned to eat from a human hand, had distemper shots, lain curled by a fire on a winter's night, or slept at the foot of a child's bed. It must have had a name.

Lucky? Big Red? What would a dog like that be called? Junior? Each of the dogs had had masters, walked on leashes and children to play with. What had happened to bring them to this front yard? What had turned them into vicious killers? For undeniably that was what they were.

There were eleven of them, all big dogs save the dachshund. They sat motionless in the snow watching the house. Only the dachshund was not content. It hopped around frenetically from dog to dog, sniffing, pushing, playing by itself in a far section of the yard. At first Larry could not see what the dog was playing with. It appeared to be a toy of some sort which the dog continually picked up, gnawed at, then dropped into the snow again. He tried to focus clearly, to see what it was, but the dog stayed in the dark. Finally, the dachshund took the object in his teeth and rolled over into the light, still chewing diligently. And suddenly Larry realized what the dog was playing with. Retching, he leaned over the sink.

In the center of the pack, the shepherd waited. Although his night vision was far superior to that of daylight, when too much light almost blinded him, the shepherd did not see Larry at the window until he moved. The motion attracted the dog's attention, but even then he could not be sure this was his enemy. He was aware only of an ill-defined shape silhouetted in the window.

Larry leaned on his arms, sobbing. Fucking, rotten, stinking, bastards! He wanted to kill them all, destroy them. His eyes swept through the room, seeking a weapon. Anything capable of inflicting pain would serve.

But instead his eyes fixed on the bloody body of the Airedale. In two strides he was at the body. He would show them. He took hold of the wiry-haired tail at its base, and dragged the body across the floor. Her insides trailed along behind the body, leaving a thin line of blood and small bits of gut.

Opening the kitchen door wide, he moved out onto the low wooden step. He had no fear of the pack now. Turning his back on them, he grabbed the tail with both hands, and yanked the body out into the snow.

Murmuring curses, Larry tried to lift the body by its tail. His intent was to launch it into the air to show them his strength. But the body weighed an unwieldy forty pounds, too much for him to fling very far. He was forced to settle for a half spin, and the carcass tumbled into the yard, splattering the snow with blood.

Larry stood triumphantly on the step, looking into the dark, almond-shaped eyes of the gray shepherd. Now they knew he was not afraid of them. He had proved he could face them. He would wage this battle and win.

The shepherd stared back defiantly. His meaning was clear. He would fight to the death.

The siege had begun.

SIX

Arctic cold moved in with the great winter storm that struck the mainland, and the dogs suffered through the night. The frigid air froze the damp that clung to their coats, and periodically they had to shake themselves free of the small icicles that formed. As the night grew colder some of the dogs retreated to the forest where the thick trunks of the aged trees protected them from the wind.

The shepherd did not move. This was his first night without his mate. Her body, now partially covered by the blowing snow, still lay beyond the wooden bridge. But his enemy was separated from him by impossible barriers. Eventually he would come out, and when he did, the gray dog would be waiting.

Inside the house Larry concentrated on constructing a barricade. They were not going to get in again. He had found a hammer and nails and some lengths of board.

After slipping a firm piece of cardboard into the broken windowpane, he'd nailed all of the first-floor windows shut. Then he placed a long board across the living room door and nailed that secure. Dogs are very strong, he thought as he worked. He couldn't remember exactly which breeds, or where he'd learned it, but he absolutely knew that certain dogs were capable of great feats of strength.

But they would not break into his house. He would see to that. He held another long board vertically against the kitchen wall, between the sink and the door, and hammered a nail into it. Now, if the dogs attacked all he would have to do was swing the board horizontally and quickly hammer a few more nails into it. That would reinforce the door. Meanwhile, they would have a way to leave the house in an emergency. As he worked he listened for any sound from outside.

They were intelligent, these dogs, Larry thought. Not as smart as a man, but still pretty damn smart. They had to be. They'd survived half a brutal winter, organized into a pack, and obeyed a leader. Smart. He remembered all the heroic dogs he had seen perform; Rin Tin Tin, he was another shepherd, shepherds seemed to be the smartest dogs; Lassie, the collie, she was pretty smart, too. Then there was Roy Rogers' dog, another shepherd, whatever his name was. And so many others. He knew their exploits weren't real, he knew they didn't *really* perform those feats, but he also recognized that they were capable of learning innumerable tricks. Smart animals. Guide dogs, he suddenly remembered, probably the smartest of all. Took the place of eyes. And they were usually shepherds, too.

After sealing up the downstairs he checked the second floor, deciding to leave only the window at the end of the hall open. It was too high for the dogs to reach, and they could use some fresh air in the house. Finally, when he was sure the house was secure, he started checking on the people within.

Corny was smiling as he entered the bedroom. Sitting in the middle of the floor leafing through an old issue of *Life* magazine, she looked up at Larry as if nothing were wrong. "Hi, Corny," he said warmly.

His mother was still asleep, her face half-buried in a feather pillow. Corny stopped turning the pages and watched him as he went across the room and pulled a heavy quilt over Frieda's frail shoulders. He hoped she would not dream.

"Are you all right, Corny?" he asked.

She frowned. "I'm fine. But my daddy said I couldn't go out and play with the dogs."

He realized Corny's mind was still refusing to accept the truth, rejecting the horror, projecting her back to a pleasanter time. "Well, you stay here for a while and then we'll see what happens," he said as naturally as he could. But as he left the room he made sure the door was securely closed.

The children were both fast asleep, cupped against each other. In the half-light Diane sat in a wicker chair working over her nails. She did not look up when he entered the room. He knew it was important that they speak now, before the barriers between them could become solidified, but he didn't know how to begin. "You okay?"

"I'm okay." She concentrated on her shining nails, carefully shaping them with an emery board. The battle in the kitchen seemed far away.

Larry needed to talk about it. "I'm uh. . . ." The words still would not come. "I've sealed up the downstairs," he mumbled, "they can't get in."

The hall light reflected off the bedroom wall, enabling her to make out his face. He was still a handsome man, still young. Successful. He had faithfully fulfilled his part of their marriage vows. Diane took a deep breath. "I'm sorry, Larry," she apologized without warmth, almost by rote, "I lost control."

"You're all right now, though?"

"I guess so."

"The kids?" He spoke quietly in order not to wake them.

"They're okay." Every sentence was a chore. She was being careful not to upset him. Their marriage was probably not in jeopardy, she realized, just their relationship.

"The dogs are in the yard," he told her. It was not at all what he wanted to say. But somehow it was what came out and sat heavily on the air.

Diane had heard their cries, too, and was not surprised they had returned. It was as if she'd expected it, almost as if it were inevitable. "Is there anything . . . something I can do?"

What? What could she possibly do, he wondered bitterly. Call a meeting of the dogs and vote on whether they should menace the house? Organize a fund raiser? His anger was close to the surface, but he dismissed it. "No, nothing. Just watch the kids."

"If there is anything—" she started hopefully.

He cut her off. "Yeah, I know."

There was nothing more to say. He started to pull the door shut, but she stopped him abruptly. "Larry?"

"What?" This time his voice was tinged with irritability.

Diane's voice broke in midsentence as she begged him, "Can't you get us out of here?"

She sounded so helpless, a tone he recognized. "Yeah," he tried to tell her, but the word stuck in his throat. He coughed it clear, and told her he would try. Then he closed the door and went back down the stairs.

Diane sat in the darkness of the room with her sleeping

children. As she manicured the middle nail on her left hand she discovered the beginning of a small crack, and wondered if she'd remembered to pack that silly nail cement.

Help. So much had happened so quickly Larry hadn't had time to think about summoning help. First Corny, then his father, then the fight in the kitchen, and finally the need to secure the house. But now, in his first free moments, he realized that they did indeed need outside aid. Someone to prevent the dogs from getting at his family, to keep them from killing again, to destroy the pack. He could do it himself, he admitted, with the right weapons. A gun would be fine, but the Winchester had been smashed. There were some knives, but using them would mean in-close fighting, and he couldn't risk that.

What if the dogs should attack again before help could arrive? With the house barricaded he figured they were safe temporarily, but what if the dogs got in, what would he do then? Fight them, of couse, but with what? The knives? They wouldn't be enough. There had to be a real weapon somewhere in the house. But he found nothing in any of the closets, nothing hidden under the sink, nothing in the long window box. And the Winchester, Larry knew, had been the only firearm his father permitted in the house.

His entire arsenal consisted of three long kitchen knives, the hammer, and the broken blade of a handsaw found in the tool drawer. Carefully he distributed these weapons about the first floor. The longest knife he left in the kitchen. He placed a second knife on the fireplace mantel, and the third on a high table near the staircase, in the improbable event he was forced to retreat upstairs. He shoved the hammer into his belt. Temporarily, at least, he would carry it with him. Then he carefully taped the broken saw blade, cutting edge up, across the bottom of the broken kitchen window. If the pack tried to get in that way a sharp surprise would be awaiting them. Finally, he picked up the long heavy metal coal shovel that hung beside the fireplace and left it on the kitchen counter. Now, he thought, if they come, I'll be ready for them.

The dogs remained in the front yard, sitting quietly, waiting. Like the implacable stone lions in front of the New York Public Library, Larry decided.

But waiting for what? Why had they come back? Food? Impossible. He shuddered. Revenge? Absolutely not. The dogs were smart, at least that shepherd was smart, but even he could not possess that much reasoning power. Then, for what? And for how long?

Waiting was going to be difficult, that was obvious. His wounds ached but the bleeding had stopped, and he did not seem to have suffered serious damage. It was the tension that would get to them eventually. The fact of the dogs' presence was overwhelming. They were visible in the yard from numerous windows, and the awful threat they represented could not be ignored. Eventually, Larry knew, living with that threat would become unbearable.

He realized now that he had to get professional help. No one in the house was capable of aiding him. The children were too young, his mother too old, Corny too far gone, and Diane? Diane was simply incapable. If he couldn't take care of the dogs himself, he would need other men, armed men, to destroy the pack.

Then why hadn't he already called the police? It would be easier and much safer to let them handle the dogs. Why hadn't he? Easing his body down into Thomas Hardman's comfortable chair, he probed his mind for the answer. Revenge? Revenge for what they had done to Charlie Cornwall and to his father? Certainly that was partially true. Was it Frieda? Yes, that too. Fear? Yes. Eventually it would be discovered that he had run away while his father was being mauled. He would have to learn to live with that. It would be difficult, he realized, but possible. Destroying the pack by himself would make it easier.

Machismo, that was the reason. His desperate need to prove that he, alone, could protect his family. His need to prove that one man is superior to a pack of witless animals, that one human mind can outwit any number of dogs. Thus far, though, he had failed. His father's death was evidence of his failure. So he would have to destroy them, or live forever with his defeat.

He would kill them, and that would show her.

The thought startled him. Her? Diane? Diane loved him, there was no question of that. Maybe he had indulged her too much over the years, maybe he hadn't been as demanding as he should have been. But now he would show her. Now he would reestablish his superiority.

There was more. He tried to shut off his mind, but it pumped out additional truths. The reason surfaced no matter how he denied it. Finally he had to admit to himself that the night's excitement had exhilarated him far beyond anything in recent memory. That he once again felt incredibly alive after so many dead years in the city.

He wasn't ready to give up that wondrous feeling. Could it possibly be as simple as that? The adventure of life and death. Would he dare risk the lives of his family for that? He could not answer.

Diane stretched her long legs in the narrow bed, careful not to disturb the dreams of her children. Sleep would not come. Instead a flood of thoughts raced through her mind. Larry, the dogs, the children, the problem of finding a new maid to replace the Haitian who had quit after being yelled at, Larry again. And always.

He was not a fighter. Too sensitive, perhaps even

insecure, although there was little reason for him to be. He had a pretty wife, she would admit to being pretty, a prosperous career, and numerous friends. How much of this she was responsible for Diane did not really know. Some, she decided, and left it at that.

Larry had a lot to be happy about. She had done her best to make their marriage work. She'd given him two lovely children and invariably subjugated her own interests to his career. But it wasn't enough. At some point their marriage had stopped working. She fell asleep trying to figure out exactly what had gone wrong.

It took a full ten seconds for a somewhat hazy dial tone to clock on. Larry dialed operator and waited while the phone rang. Seven times. Nine times. The underwater cable that connected the island to the mainland had been laid in 1957 and, except in the worst weather, communication was usually good. Fourteen. Fifteen. Six. . . .

"Operator."

"This is an emergency, operator. Get me the police, please."

More clicks. Rings. Six. Seven. Eight. Over the buzzing in his ear he listened for sounds from the yard. Maybe they'd left.

An exhausted resonant voice interrupted his thought. "Suffolk County Police. Sergeant Stromfeld."

What could he tell them? That a pack of wild dogs were terrorizing a house full of people? It sounded . . . ridiculous. Dogs?

"Hello?"

He cleared his throat. "Yes. Excuse me, officer. My name is Larry Hardman. I'm calling from—"

"Can you speak up, please? I can't hear you too good."

He spoke up. "This is Larry Hardman, and I'm calling you from Burrows Island." He paused to take a deep breath, then lost his poise completely. "They killed my father," he cried, "and another man, a neighbor. There's a pack of wild dogs on the island. . . ."

"Hold it, hold it a second. What did you say? Who killed 'em?"

"Dogs," Larry said clearly, "the dog pack." Why couldn't he understand? "They're in the yard. . . ."

Sergeant Stromfeld shifted in the wooden swing-chair as he listened to the fantastic story unwind. The caller, Harding, Hardman, whatever, wasn't particularly lucid, and some of his facts seemed confused, but it was obvious they were having problems on Burrows Island. "How many dead did you say there were?" he interrupted.

"At least two," Larry told him. "There's another neighbor we can't get hold of. He doesn't answer his phone."

"And dogs killed them?"

"I know it sounds unbelievable, but. . . ."

Sergeant Stromfeld had proudly served the good people of Suffolk County for twelve years. He'd cleaned up after plane wrecks at MacArthur Field, gathered pieces of bodies that floated up after weeks in the water, carried the smashed bodies of children who had been hit by cars in his arms and once even rescued a pet canary from a gar-bage disposal unit. He'd made two bank robbery arrests, ticketed innumerable reckless drivers, found dozens of lost kids and broken up more domestic arguments than he could keep track of. In these twelve years he'd drawn his gun nineteen times, fired warning shots twice, and shot once to bring down his target. That had been a payroll robber and, thankfully, his shot had missed. He'd also had his share of dog problems; potentially rabid, run over, lost, dead, and mad. He'd seen dogs leap from moving vehicles, attack on command, and once, go after a child. But he had never, ever seen or heard of a dog actually killing a human being. And he wasn't sure he really considered it possible. "Where are the dogs now?" he asked when Larry Hardman finished.

"They're sitting in the front yard."

Sergeant Stromfeld paused. "They're what?"

"Sitting out there, there are eleven of them watching the house."

"Why?" Sergeant Stromfeld tried to keep the tone of his voice from betraying his disbelief.

"Look," Larry said irritably, "I don't know what they want. And I know this is all hard to believe. But they're out there, believe me, sitting and waiting . . ."

Early morning drunken phone calls were inherent with the graveyard shift. Flying Volkswagens, escaped lions, Martian landings, Adolf Hitler on the Long Island Expressway and, after the film, *The Exorcist,* there had been a rash of possessions by the Devil. These were the usual things, almost expected. Stromfeld didn't think the guy sounded drunk, but man-killing dogs sitting calmly in the front yard were hard to accept. He had a dog of his own, Fumfer, a collie, and he didn't believe she was capable of pinching a backyard squirrel much less killing a human being.

Still, the book called for him to handle each call politely and professionally, whatever his personal opinion might be. He swung his chair around and checked the duty roster hanging on the peeling green wall behind him. The storm had really screwed up everything. Half the guys couldn't get to work, and the half who were on duty had been working so long they were asleep on their feet. "Hold it one minute, Mr. Harding," he told Larry, "I'm checking something." The only way out to the island was by boat or helicopter. The seas had been too choppy all week for small boats, and the bigger boats were working on that damned grounded tanker. The gusting hurricane force winds prevented the use of the choppers.

Larry waited patiently on the other end of the telephone. The police would not be able to help, he knew that. . . .

"Mr. Harder, sorry to keep you waiting, but I'm just trying to figure out how we can help you. See we got an emergency of our own here. Power lines down, drivers marooned in vehicles and at least two serious gas leaks we're trying to get the Lilco people to seal up."

Larry heard an almost melodic bark outside. They were still there. "What does all that mean?"

The sergeant did not answer him directly. "Here's what I want you to do. I want you to tell me exactly where your house is located on the island, and as soon as we get a break in the weather, I'll get some people over to you. But as long as you stay in the house, I don't think you'll be in any real danger. Is that clear?"

Too clear. There was no help to be expected from the police. "How long do you think it'll be before somebody gets here?"

"Jesus," Sergeant Stromfeld said, looking up at the fluorescent lights as if for an answer. "I wish I could tell you. Maybe two days, give or take a little. It's still snowing like hell here, you know."

Larry did not know that. And didn't care. Two days! Doing his best to hold his temper, he gave Sergeant Stromfeld specific directions to the house. "And tell your people they better bring some rifles."

Stromfeld wrote that down on his memo pad. "I'll tell them that, sir."

"Listen. Is there anybody else who might be able to help us sooner?"

Stromfeld consulted his directory of emergency services. "You might try the Coast Guard," he suggested. "But I'd advise you to stay in the house. You've got to be safe that way, don't you?"

"Sure, thanks," Larry said, trying not to sound sarcastic.

"And check the doors to make sure they're closed tight so nothing can get in." Sympathizing with the crazies made it easier to get them off the phone.

"Thanks," Larry repeated. And slammed the phone down.

Stromfeld wrote out a brief report of the call and passed it along to the dispatcher. She would put it on her schedule and send the first available men over to the island once the seas calmed down. Personally, Stromfeld believed the trip would prove a waste of time, but there was nothing he could do, it was all part of the job.

The gray shepherd got to his feet and began inspecting the line of dogs. The pack had huddled in pairs for warmth. Now they began to stir. The boxer sniffed in the snow for a proper place to urinate. The dog moved close to the house, then along it, lifting his leg periodically. The other dogs watched impassively, the meaning was clear. The boxer was marking territory.

A moment later the collie followed him, taking over beyond the boxer, and extended the line. A little later the golden retriever repeated the ritual. As the light of morning began filtering into the yard, each of the dogs added to this barrier. Just as their ancestors had done thousands of years earlier, and their wild forest relations continued to do, the pack claimed its territory. The line of urine surrounded half the house.

The shepherd's attention centered wholly on the house. Inside, he understood, was the enemy. The pack would not be safe until this threat no longer existed. The pack would wait.

The Labrador was the last to awake. In his sleep he had been dreaming of the warmth his masters had provided for him. Now as he rose, his left leg was throbbing. When he was seventeen months old he'd chased a car, and its rear wheel had broken his left rear leg. The leg healed over a summer, but on very cold nights it still pained him. The temperature was 23 degrees F. this morning, and he could not walk off the pain.

Diane was dozing when Larry walked into the room. Fragments of light were beginning to seep through the window and he was checking the house. Leaning down over her, Larry brushed a kiss across her lips. "I do love you," he whispered and walked from the room.

Although she heard his words, and felt his kiss, she kept her eyes closed tightly and said nothing.

Larry was not at all surprised that the Coast Guard could not help either. They were already overtaxed searching for survivors from the freighter that had run aground, and trying to answer distress calls from other craft in trouble in the storms. Two days, the dispatcher told him, stay inside until then. And don't worry, he added, they're "just dogs."

Larry thanked him, cradling the phone resignedly. There would be no help from outside. He'd tried, he had made an honest effort. His wife could never challenge him on that. It was up to him. All up to him. He liked that. All up to him.

The light of dawn showed behind the ominous storm clouds when he sat down and began to work on his plan. His approach was methodical, the problem essentially an engineering one: how do you move six people from point A to point B, bypassing an immovable obstacle, with limited resources? A not so unique problem. The type he'd solved innumerable times. Absolutely solvable.

The first thing to take into consideration. . . . He hesitated. What if he failed?

He was not going to fail. There was no room for failure in this design. Once the proper conveyance for escape was determined it was. . . .

But what if he did? What if something broke, or something totally unforeseen and unpredictable happened? Who would save his children? And the women, his wife and his mother and Corny?

Calmly he analyzed all aspects of the problem. It was his profession to make sure the unpredictable was predicted and planned for within the design. Windsway. Storm centers. Pressure areas. Gas leaks. Even earthquakes, and fires. That's what he did for a living. That's why those giant buildings he put up remained standing.

But if. . . . The people in the house were his responsibility. He was the man, and therefore, by historical definition, the burden was his.

As soon as he realized this, he also understood the corollary that he could not go out into the snow again. Because of the other people in the house, he could not risk his own life.

Therefore, there was nothing to do but wait for help to arrive. It was the logical answer to the problem. He was, at the same time, sorry about that, and smugly content.

But waiting was terribly difficult. If only I had a gun, he thought. One rifle. I could stay inside the house and pick them off one by one. But he had no rifle.

Kenny had a rifle. Lots of rifles, in fact. And Kenny knew dogs. Really knew them. Kenny could help.

Larry turned the brand new thought over carefully in his mind. Kenny, kid brother Kenny, was an absolute gun nut. No, not nut, he corrected himself, gun expert. Kenny could break down and reassemble any hand weapon manufactured. Guns were his hobby. He'd won all kinds of gun medals in Vietnam. And he'd always had dogs, hunting dogs, of course, but dogs.

It was funny how different two brothers could be, Larry thought. One, a gentle man. The other held hunting licenses from more states than he could probably remember. One, a responsible, respected member of the community. The other. . . . Larry felt charitable. The other hadn't found his career interest yet. He was a wanderer. But he was a wanderer who could damn well shoot straight.

Where the hell was he now? Larry tried to remember the last phone call. Somewhere up in Connecticut. He could find the number. And Kenny could make it to the island. He was a hunter and this sort of weather would be a challenge to him. He'd gather some friends, they'd rent a boat, come across to the island and pick the dogs off. They could do it!

All he had to do was pick up the phone and call Kenny. It was that simple. One phone call to his kid brother and within hours they would be safe. Larry sat staring at the phone. But could not bring himself to pick it up.

The golden retriever tried to shake off the morning chill, then walked back over the wooden bridge into the woods. The shepherd watched him go, leaving a hole in the line, but did nothing. The retriever would be back.

The dog went back into the forest, following the scent toward the body of Thomas Hardman.

SEVEN

Frieda Hardman stood by her bedroom window looking down on the dogs. From her vantage point she noticed how intelligently they had spaced themselves out in the yard. Almost human, she thought. She watched two of the dogs romping in the snow, playing with something. It was too far to see what it was.

Her thoughts went to her husband. She knew he was dead. She allowed herself no illusions, no false hopes, she was too realistic for that, but she did refuse to let her mind wonder about his death. She would not think of his torn body. Instead, she would remember him as he lived, gritty and proud. Thomas Hardman had given her a good life, she had been happy in their marriage, and believed he had been happy, too.

As she watched the dogs playing, she noticed a shred of red plaid material caught on a bush. She accepted the fact that the remnant was from his shirt, and might be the only evidence of his fate she would ever see.

Corny was quite busy cutting brightly colored photographs from the old magazine, and thus did not even notice her friend was out of bed. For one moment Frieda considered joining her on the floor, but the pills clogged her head and made her tired, so that she had to lie down and close her eyes again.

"Are they coming?" Diane walked into the kitchen and addressed the question to Larry's back. He was leaning against the sink, watching the pack.

"Who?" He did not turn around. The dogs continued to bewilder him. They stayed in position in the yard, quietly, contentedly even, seemingly waiting, oblivious to the cold, as if they possessed some irrefutable knowledge of a future victory.

"The Army. The Navy. I don't know, whoever you called before."

The shepherd was the most unusual of them all. It was not necessarily his looks, the dog was thin in the flank and its coat was matted. Rather it was the absolute control he held over the rest of the pack. There was little doubt in Larry's mind that the dog communicated intelligently with the other animals. But how? And why this one dog? What made it so special? "The Suffolk County Police," he answered, "and the United States Coast Guard. And no, they're not coming." He corrected himself. "At least not right away."

Diane opened one of the cabinets above the refrigerator to look for a jar of instant coffee. Instead she found a pound of blend. Naturally, she thought bitterly, only the real thing. She put it back, taking the pitcher of squeezed orange juice from the refrigerator. After pouring a glass she took a seat at the kitchen table, still facing her husband's back. "Larry," she said firmly, "I want you to. . . ." She paused. "Will you please turn around and talk to me?"

Diane's puffy white face glared at him. He noticed faint purple shadows under her wide eyes, and was suddenly aware how rarely he saw her without makeup.

"Why aren't they coming?" she demanded.

"They are not coming," he said, distinctly pronouncing each word, "because they are overloaded with problems from the storm. Apparently they don't consider us in immediate danger." He wondered about the storm hitting the mainland so hard. That itself was a neat bit of irony. A big snowstorm was exactly what was needed to drive the dogs away from the house, to force them into the forest for protection. So what happens? A major snowstorm just brushes by the island, just touches it with a few inches, the first storm in . . . in who knew how many years to miss the island. Why? Again, he had no answer, just an uneasy feeling.

"What are we going to do?"

Larry noted that her voice was remarkably controlled, considering her normal temperament. Wait, he told her. Wait until the Suffolk County Police have picked up all their downed power lines, or the Coast Guard has pulled every last survivor from the swelling seas.

He was very much in control this morning, she decided. Looking at him, she was reminded of her own appearance, and wondered just how dreadful she looked. Normally, the first thing she did each morning was put on her makeup. But this morning, this one morning, that hadn't even entered her mind. But now, thinking about it, she was positive she looked an absolute mess. Her hair just had to resemble a fright wig. The makeup she'd put on for dinner the night before, just a touch of eye color and a quick brush of rouge, was long since gone. And since she hadn't been near the club in days her tan was at best yellow, if not altogether faded. She attempted to put her hair in order with her hands, then stopped. It doesn't matter, she thought, it really doesn't matter.

Larry was amazed at how good he felt considering yesterday's horrors and his sleepless night. The bright beauty of the new morning seemed to give the lie to everything he knew to be true. He felt in control. He welcomed the advantage of clear vision that the daylight granted him. He felt emotionally renewed. In the morning light everything seemed possible.

His muscles still ached, and his hand throbbed, but these were the pains of survival and he refused to let them bother him. How do I feel? he asked himself. Alive, he answered. Admittedly, he'd gotten tired toward dawn, but the sunlight woke him. What he really needed was a cup of coffee, clean clothes and a shave. He'd shave over the sink, he decided, and keep watch on the dogs. "The thing that really interests me," he said as he poured his own glass of juice, "is the fact that they're not moving. They're not doing anything at all. I don't know much about dogs, but I know that's not normal."

There were eggs in the refrigerator, but he'd already ruled out cooking anything that might create a scent. No reason to get them excited out there. They would make do with cold food.

From the table, Diane could not see out the window. That was fine with her, she'd been doing her best to put the dogs out of her mind. And out of sight, out of mind. At least that seemed to work for her. It made life less confusing only to deal with problems when they finally became unavoidable. "Why don't you call Kenny?" she suggested, knowing that would get her husband's attention.

Looking out at them again, Larry decided they did not look so vicious. The dachshund appeared funny, as dachshunds are supposed to be. The golden retriever beautiful, much like the bitch Kenny owned when they were children. The Labrador friendly, a big handsome dog, a smiling dog. And the shepherd? In some perverse way, gallant. In the fresh light of morning it was difficult to believe these animals were capable of such destruction.

Call Kenny? Her question hung in the air as he watched the pack. "I thought about it, you know, I really did. I even found his number in Dad's book. But I didn't call him." He shrugged his shoulders. "I don't know why."

You do, she thought.

Yes, I do, he thought.

Diane had never been able to understand why these brothers had grown up to be so different. Larry was only three years older than Kenny; they were close enough in age so that they should have had something in common. But there was nothing. They were different people, opposites, at once jealous and resentful of each other. She'd first seen it the day they had gotten engaged. The moment Kenny walked into Larry's East Side apartment the subtle put-down had begun. At first she had attributed Kenny's attitude to a lack of character, later she understood it lay at the heart of his relationship to Larry.

Actually, she did not like Kenny very much, and so was glad he stayed away. But at this moment she believed he could help them. And that was enough reason to make Larry call him. "I want you to call him," she said flatly.

Larry turned from the window. She was right. Kenny could help. In fact, Kenny would love to come and rescue them. It would support his feelings of primacy. "Diane."

It was the beginning of a plea. "I'd like—" He got no further.

His answer was cut off by the sound of glass smashing, and an instant later by a shrill, panic-stricken scream. "The children," Diane began, but Larry had already seized the small fireplace shovel and was at the stairs. In three long strides he reached the first-floor landing. The door to the children's room was locked, but Larry heard scuffling sounds from within. Taking a half step backward he kicked the door open with his right foot and was in the room before the doorknob crashed into the wall.

Josh and Marcy stopped their wrestling match and looked up at him. "What's the matter, Dad?" Josh asked.

Marcy giggled, repeating her older brother's question. "Wassa mabber, Dad?"

"Stay here," he ordered, "don't leave this room." He pulled the door closed and almost slammed into Diane as he turned toward the second bedroom. "Stay with them," he ordered curtly.

Swiftly he crossed the hall to his mother's room. As he reached the door another scream came from inside. It was Corny's voice. He raised the shovel, then pushed the door open.

Corny was on the floor. In front of her lay an overturned sewing basket, and dozens of buttons of all colors, shapes and sizes, littered the floor. She was smiling and, as he stood staring at her, she screamed once again. Then laughed.

Frieda was not in the room. "Where's my mother?" Larry asked as gently as he could. "Where is she?" Corny laughed again.

"I'm right here," Frieda Hardman said wearily as she rose from behind the bed, large pieces of the old table lamp in her hand. "I knocked this down," she said apologetically.

"Are you okay?"

"I'm fine, son."

He nodded toward Corny. "And her?"

His mother answered with a long, sad, helpless look. "Larry, I. . . ." She paused. "I don't know what to do. We need. . . . She needs. . . ."

"I know, Ma, I know. It's okay, help is coming soon. I called Kenny. He's coming to help us. He'll be here as soon as he can," Larry lied.

Frieda's face brightened at the mention of her younger son. "Thank goodness."

"He told me to tell you that he loves you very much."

She smiled, but did not answer.

"Are you really all right?"

She understood what he was asking. "Yes, son, I'm all right. I'm just worried about. . . ." Corny's name was left unspoken. "Isn't there anything we can do?"

"Soon, Ma, soon. I promise. Just stay in here with her. Don't leave her alone." He started to leave, then stopped at the door. "You want another pill?"

Frieda indicated a bottle on the small night table. "Diane left these with me. I'll take one later."

"Maybe you should give one to Corny to quiet her down." Corny did not even lift her head at the mention of her name.

His mother nodded agreement, and Larry closed the door. The complete confidence he felt moments ago was gone; instead, now he felt overwhelming exhaustion.

A crisp voice spoke into the telephone. "Yeah?"

"Kenny? It's Larry."

There was a brief pause before Kenny responded. "Well, big brother, how the hell are you? Long time no hear."

Larry tried to picture his brother on the other end of the phone. He guessed that Kenny was smiling at the call. "I know. I'm sorry to call you so early in the morning but"—he stopped abruptly, then blurted out—"look, I need your help." There, it was done, Larry thought. And now, he was sure, his brother's smile would be growing.

Kenny's voice was alert, and Larry figured he'd been awake for some time. In fact, he had hardly been to sleep. When the telephone rang he was sharing his mattress-on-the-floor with a pubescent blonde named either Laura or Linda, he wasn't quite sure which, whom he'd known for almost twelve hours. Two drained bottles of Almaden Chablis, roaches of four joints, and the rumpled blankets and sheets attested to the intensity of their growing friendship. Now, in his usual flippant voice he asked his older brother exactly what was wrong.

Larry spaced his words carefully. "I'm on the island, Kenny, with Diane and the children." He paused again, wondering how best to proceed. In dealing with Kenny, he knew, plowing straight ahead usually worked best. "Dad's dead," he reported as unemotionally as possible.

Silence. Then, a disbelieving "What?" The flippancy was gone from the voice.

"Dad's dead, Kenny. Look, I don't know. . . ."

"Wait a second. Just one second." Kenny tried to clear the residue of the night from his mind. "What happened?" The girl caught the change in his tone and sat up next to him.

Larry did his best to keep his voice even. "I don't know exactly how to explain what's happened here, but there's a dog pack on the island and the dogs just. . . ." Larry had to stop and take a deep breath before continuing.

The blonde had begun stroking Kenny's massive, hairy back. Twisting sideways, he thrust her hand away. "You mean wolves, don't you? You don't mean dogs."

"I *mean* dogs," Larry replied firmly. "Look, I told you it was hard to believe, but. . . ."

"Larry," Kenny patiently began explaining, "they couldn't be dogs. Not on Burrows Island at least. See, dogs were pack animals once, but they've lost that instinct. Now they're too jealous of each other, they fight over everything. Except for a few hunting breeds, dogs don't mix."

As Larry listened to his brother's lecture, his anger and frustration brewed to a boil. Finally, when he could take it no longer, he exploded. "Goddamn it, I'm not an idiot," he screamed into the phone, slamming his fist into the table. "I'm telling you what I saw with my own eyes. I don't care how it sounds, but there's a pack of dogs sitting in the front yard trying to get into this house. And they killed your father, and Charlie Cornwall and . . . and . . ." He heard himself yelling, and stopped. "I'm sorry, Kenny, it's just. . . ."

Kenny accepted the apology. "I know, Larry."

"Yeah," Larry grunted as he tried to recover his demeanor.

Calmly, Kenny began asking Larry specific questions. "What breeds are they?"

Larry looked through the kitchen and out the window as he answered. "All different ones. A shepherd, boxer, dalmatian, there's a Labrador, a couple I'm not sure of, a dachshund. . . ."

The pack of mixed breeds, as Larry described them, didn't seem possible, but Kenny knew his brother could identify dogs, even if he couldn't handle them.

". . . Dad said they were abandoned by summer tourists. I don't know, I guess they must have formed this pack to survive."

"Can you tell what dog is the leader?" The blonde stretched out beside him, and began rubbing her own smooth body.

"It's a shepherd, a gray shepherd."

Kenny ignored her totally. "That figures."

"Why?"

"Shepherds are really bright dogs, maybe the brightest. And it would take a really unusual dog to hold a mixed breed pack together. How big is this one?"

Larry stared at the gray dog lazing in the snow. "About eighty pounds, I guess, I can't tell for sure."

"Well, that's not too bad. I've seen 'em up to a hundred and fifty pounds. Listen, are there red bones or black and tans out there?" He hoped not.

"I'm not sure, I don't think so. Why?" He felt so helpless, so much at Kenny's mercy.

"Just curious. No real reason." Except the fact that these were the great hunting breeds. They had the best nose, the best sight, and were strong and smart, Kenny knew. Added to the intelligence of the shepherd, they would be a formidable match for any human being. "Now Larry, just tell me what happened."

"They attacked Charlie Cornwall first, just dragged him away from his house. When Dad and I—"

"Why'd they attack?" The blonde, bored with being ignored, rose from the mattress and began slipping gold satin panties over her long legs. Without losing an instant of concentration, Kenny reached over and grabbed them, preventing her from putting them on.

"Who knows? Hunger, I guess." He debated for a moment telling Kenny about the early afternoon shooting, then decided against it.

"What happened exactly?"

"When Dad and I went to try to find him, they attacked." As he spoke the seemingly simple words, Larry felt as if he were confessing a terrible sin. "And they just"— he squeezed his fist tightly, driving his nails into his palm, as he tried desperately to explain—"they just killed him, Kenny."

Kenny released his grip on the gold panties, and the blonde slowly pulled them on. "Weren't you there?" he asked softly.

" 'Course I was there."

"And you couldn't help him? For God's sake," Kenny said, his voice steadily rising with each word, "he was an old man."

Larry pleaded for understanding. "I tried, Kenny, I fought them. I killed one or two of them. But the Winchester snapped in half and they had him on the ground. There wasn't anything I could do, I swear it, Kenny, there was nothing I could do. I tried, I really tried. . . ." His plea for compassion rolled furiously out of his mouth.

Kenny caught his own breath, then tried to calm his older brother. It wouldn't help anybody if Larry lost control of himself. "It's okay, big brother," he said in a forced, jocular voice, "take it easy." He waited a moment, then asked, "How's Mom taking it?"

It was another moment before Larry could compose himself to speak again. "She seems all right. We're all in the house and I've got it locked tight. I don't think they can get in, do you?"

Kenny did not answer immediately.

"You don't, do you?" Larry asked in a more urgent voice.

If they were hungry enough, dogs were capable of anything, he knew. They were capable of smashing through a window, or pounding a door into pieces, or even gnawing through it. He was silently thankful the pack contained no black and tans or red bones, with their extraordinary sense of smell. "Nah," he finally answered easily, "they can't get in the house, ole buddy boy. You're just as snug as a bug in a rug, till I get my sweet body over there."

This is a mistake, Larry thought, as he listened to his brother's feigned coolness, *I never should have called him. I should have done it myself, I should have killed them myself. He must love listening to me plead for his help.*

Long-hidden feelings of shame came rushing back into his mind, feelings he thought had been buried deep in his memory. Kenny carrying him home from the gorge after he tripped and broke his foot, Kenny pulling him from a fight and pummeling the other battler, Kenny scurrying up the giant oak tree to free a tangled kite, Kenny diving into the Sound and dragging him out of a dangerous current. Kenny, always Kenny. How he hated that! The day he left the island he swore he would never need Kenny again. And now he was forced to ask this gun-toting social scrounger to come to his rescue, and he loathed that.

Kenny too understood the implications of the call. He knew Larry saw him as a wastrel; a worthless drifter, floating from town to town, job to job, woman to woman. Immature, he had called him the last time they spoke. Wasting your life, he'd screamed. But now he was asking for help, and Kenny savored the moment.

Later he would mourn his father, but his thoughts then were on the promised adventure of shooting some wild dogs and this opportunity to prove Larry wrong. "So you just sit tight there and I'll grab two guys and we'll get over there as fast as we can."

"I don't have to remind you to bring your guns," Larry said.

"No, you don't," Kenny boasted, "remember, I'm the hunter. You're the one who lives in the city." In his mind he was already juggling logistics. "A lot of roads are out, this has been a bad storm."

"We got the fringes of it," Larry explained, ignoring Kenny's sarcasm. "It's been blowing on and off since we got here."

"With luck we can pack and make the dock by four.

Then it depends how long it takes us to find a boat. Maybe not till tomorrow morning."

"Just get here as soon as you can."

"Yes, sir, soon as I can. Now tell me the whole setup again, this time a little slower."

Once again Larry detailed the situation. And, as he was doing so, he wondered how any human being could accept the news of a parent's death so casually. It seemed so perfectly Kenny.

"Never fear," Kenny chimed when he finished, "I will be there."

Larry mumbled his appreciation and hung up. "He's coming with some friends," he told Diane wearily. "They'll be here tonight if they can find a boat to bring them over. Otherwise tomorrow."

Diane smiled, feeling an incredible wave of relief. She knew the call had been terribly difficult for him to make, so she masked her feelings carefully. There was no advantage in hurting him further. Help was on the way.

They sat in silence, together. They had never been further apart.

Kenny reached over and nudged the receiver back onto its base. The blonde was admiring herself in a wall mirror. Her high, proud breasts reflected back at Kenny but all he could think about were the dogs. He'd heard about once-domesticated dogs turning wild, even forming packs. But actually attacking human beings? Menacing a house? The pack leader, the gray shepherd, he knew, had to be an unusual dog. A frighteningly intelligent dog. A dog that he'd believed existed only in legends and lies.

She turned around to face him. "Are you going somewhere?"

"Hunting," he replied, and reached over to have her one final time.

The rich chestnut Irish setter froze, pointing to the forest, weight slightly forward, tail extended, head held high. A wolfhound rose and moved quickly across the bridge, its head low to the ground as he searched for the scent. At the edge of the woods he lifted his 120-pound bulk over the reaching branches of a fallen tree and continued tracking. Finally he picked up the scent and his pace quickened. Then the dog halted. He had spotted his prey as it floundered in the deep snow.

A large branch had broken under the weight of new snow and dumped its white load into the winter home of a small brown forest squirrel, forcing the tiny rodent to seek new shelter. The setter had picked up the sound of the crashing branch, then the scent of the squirrel, but the wolfhound had gone out after it.

At first the squirrel was apprehensive, dashing from one seemingly safe spot to another. Once it suspected motion in the forest, and frantically clawed halfway up a tree trunk to safety but after a long hesitation, decided it was safe and climbed down to resume searching.

The wolfhound lumbered twenty feet closer as the squirrel busily uncovered what it thought might be a food source. The dog froze again, its left front leg suspended in midair.

The squirrel moved again, this time farther into the open.

The wolfhound unconsciously estimated all the variables and its instinct said it could now take its prey. With incredible quickness for such a large animal it was on the squirrel before the rodent could move to escape. With a single snap its teeth clamped down on the squirrel's head. The terrified animal managed to take one swipe at the dog with its front claw before it died.

The wolfhound shook the body over and over like a rag doll. Then almost gently he put it down into the snow and raised his long pointed muzzle in an echoing song of victory.

Across the gorge, in the front yard of the Hardman house, the rest of the pack picked up the cry, raising their own voices. A symphony of baying, howling, yelping and toneless barking broke the cold silence. Louder and louder it rose, as the dogs strove to out-howl each other.

Diane joined Larry at the kitchen window. "What is it, why are they howling?" she demanded.

"I don't know." He shook his head quizzically. "I don't know what it means. Maybe they're just playing." Or maybe beginning their attack, he thought.

As she stood next to him, watching, her arm unconsciously searched for safety around his waist.

Upstairs, Josh and Marcy stood on their tiptoes and tried to look out the window. By stretching, Josh could just barely see down into the yard. "The doggies are sitting there," he proudly explained to his sister.

Dopey Dog let out an abrupt yelp. "Shut up, dumbhead," Josh said, and Dopey Dog, his tail between his legs, crept under the bed.

In the front bedroom Corny silently looked upon the scene below. Strange feelings mingled inside her. Something was definitely wrong, something that Charlie would have to fix as soon as he got home. Behind her, Frieda sat up, awakened by the pack. She tried to wipe the sleep from her eyes, surprised to find herself waking in the middle of the morning.

Kenny's euphoric yell exploded into the air. Loud and long and happy. They had packed three rifles, two full boxes of shells, two holstered handguns, six signal flares, three sleeping bags and ample food supplies into the trunk of the Land Rover. But Kenny and his two companions,

Bob Pledge and Len Hirschfeld, had been careful to keep their most important survival equipment, one entire case of cold Budweiser, in the front with them. "We're gonna shoot us some dirty dogs," Kenny boasted as he pulled the tab from the first can of Bud and maneuvered the big four-wheel drive out into the snow-clogged road.

"Take Stewart's Road," Pledge suggested, "that'll get us over to the highway quicker'n anything else." He was not at all happy about this trip. Too many roads were impassable already, and the sky was threatening more snow again. He didn't even dare guess what the weather on Long Island Sound would be like. But there just wasn't any way he could have refused after Kenny told him his family was in real danger out on whatever the hell that island's name was.

"Pass me another one of those motherloving cans of brew, if you would be so very kind," Len Hirschfeld boomed, having chugged his first can. He was determined to enjoy every moment of this entire silly trip, or at least whatever parts of it he would remember.

They plowed through a snowdrift that blocked Joan Avenue and made their way onto Stewart Street.

At a single sharp bark from the shepherd the pack fell silent.

The dogs watched as the wolfhound carried the body of the squirrel across the small bridge and laid it in the snow before the shepherd, then returned to its place in line. The shepherd sniffed the dead rodent, turned the body over with his snout, then walked out in front of the pack. And howled. Slowly, the howl was a command, the dogs stood up.

Larry shivered involuntarily. Diane's arm tightened around his waist.

"They're standing up, Marcy," Josh told his sister.

"Would you like to play a game?" Corny asked Frieda as she sat next to her on the bed, oblivious to the drama occurring below their window. "We could play Hearts."

The shepherd marched to the side of the house, out of view of Larry and Diane at the kitchen window. One by one the other dogs set off to follow him, keeping a distance of roughly twelve feet between each animal.

"Come on," Larry exclaimed, grabbing Diane's arm. They ran to a living room window to watch the shepherd.

The strange procession wound its way past their window. As he moved by, only a few feet from Larry and Diane, so close they could see the burrs caught in its pelt, the shepherd continued to stare straight ahead, giving no indication he was aware of the watchers.

By pressing his cheek against the window, Larry managed to keep the shepherd in sight until he rounded the corner of the house. With Diane close behind him, he crossed the room to the small diamond-shaped window next to the staircase.

The shepherd came into view again just as the dachshund, who had been patiently waiting in the yard, began waddling after the line.

"What's going on, Larry?" Diane asked, her voice just touching the edge of hysteria. "What's happening?"

"I don't know," he whispered. He reached into his belt and pulled out the hammer. Gripping it tightly, he realized only then that his hands were shaking badly.

The shepherd returned to the front yard as the dachshund disappeared around the first corner. Still not looking at the house, the leader kept walking his bizarre circle, passing through the yard again, trailed by the dogs of the pack.

The house, Larry realized with a great sense of foreboding, was now surrounded.

EIGHT

The dogs circled the house at a steady pace. If there seemed to be no specific purpose in their march, the sheer discipline of the action itself was enough to frighten Larry and Diane Hardman. They stationed themselves at separate window posts, Diane in the kitchen, Larry in the living room, waiting for some pause in the procession, waiting for the pack to reveal its intention.

But the dogs paraded on, ignoring the existence of the prey trapped inside, for over an hour. Then, again without any noticeable communication, the procession halted. Each dog stood in place. The gray shepherd stopped directly in front of the kitchen door, precisely the spot from which the strange walk had commenced. After a moment he lifted his muzzle and howled. To Larry the sound was somehow deeper, more sinister than it had been before. Then the other dogs joined in. The chorus was not as melodic this second time. Rather it was a clash of howls and whines and savage snarls. Hateful sounds. The sound echoed from the walls, becoming the center of the universe it created, demanding attention.

Larry saw Diane looking to him for direction. He shouted at her, "Stay here! And yell if they move toward the house!" Then he hurried up the stairs and into the bathroom. In a minute he was in the children's room. Josh and Marcy were sitting on the floor, connecting plastic bricks to make what appeared to be a tall, lopsided castle.

"What's going on, Dad?" Josh asked, an edge of nervousness in his voice.

"Yeah, Daddy," Marcy repeated, "was going on?"

"A game," he told them, "we're playing a big game with

the doggies outside." Pulling several wads of cotton from the roll he had taken from the bathroom, he explained, "Everybody has to put cotton in their ears and leave it there. Okay?"

"Can Dopey Dog have some cotton, too, Daddy?" Marcy demanded.

Dopey was lying half under the bed, his head and upper body covered by the edges of a brightly colored quilt. "I don't think he really wants any, honey. Let's ask him later."

As Larry was carefully stuffing the small balls into his children's ears, Josh asked, "How do we win?"

"It's a surprise," he answered, thinking quickly, "I don't want to ruin it for you."

Marcy wasn't very interested in the game. "I'm hungry," she whined, "Daddy, I'm hungry now."

"Soon," Larry promised, "we'll eat soon." After leaving the children he stopped at his mother's bedroom to see how the older women were reacting to the clatter. Both seemed oblivious to it. Frieda was lying on her bed, her open eyes fixed on the ceiling. Corny had returned to her spot on the floor and was carefully sewing pieces of fabric onto a blue and red woolen sweater. "Are you both all right?" Larry asked.

Frieda turned her head toward him and smiled. "Oh, we're fine." Corny sighed, without looking at him. "It's just that there's so much work to get done. We're so busy."

He left the room without another word and retreated downstairs.

The stridency of the dogs' cries had increased while he was upstairs. "They can't go on like this for too long," he said optimistically to Diane as he handed her cotton wads. After she plugged her own ears, she helped Larry stuff the cotton in his. At best, it subdued the sound somewhat.

Diane managed to prepare sandwiches for the children and the women. It was, Larry reflected, about the extent of her culinary abilities. He carefully ground up one Valium and mixed it with the children's tuna fish. Although normally he hated Diane's pills, he had to admit this time they might prove useful.

He stayed with the children while they ate, telling them a long story about dogs that he managed to invent as he went along. These dogs, he told them, big, friendly dogs, picked out one house from all those in the whole world, a house in which there was a good little boy and a good little girl, and in the middle of the night they came to that house.

Marcy looked at Josh and giggled knowingly.

The dogs, Larry went on, stayed in front of the house for a long time, barking and playing and having a good time. And when they left, in their place, the children found all sorts of wonderful presents.

"Like what?" Josh asked.

"Baseball gloves, dolls, sleds, cowboy shirts, Robby Robots, everything that would make a good little boy and a good little girl happy."

"Is that gonna happen to us?" Marcy smiled, her s's sizzling through the hole left by a missing front tooth.

"Maybe," he shrugged. "You never know until the dogs leave." Larry did not normally believe in using bribes to control children, but this would be an exception. The children would get the presents, and hopefully remember the dogs in the yard without the trauma that would otherwise accompany this terrible memory.

"I love you, Daddy," Marcy told him.

It brought him back to reality. "And I love you, honey, very much." The lock on their bedroom door had been shattered when he burst in, but the door still hung closed. On his way out he made sure it was shut as tightly as possible.

Diane made a sandwich for him and sat at the table

while he ate. At first he busied his mind trying to figure out what the pack was doing, what this crazy howling was all about. But gradually he became aware of the strain showing on his wife's face. Her eyes were watery, thin lines pulsed on her forehead and her dry lips were beginning to crack. He asked softly, "How you doin'?"

"I'm okay," she whispered.

"Aren't you going to eat?"

She shrugged her shoulders. "I'm not hungry."

"Diane," he started paternally, then realized he had no idea what he wanted to say. But after a pause he found the right words. "I don't know why they're doing this. I can't explain it, I just know it's crazy, it shouldn't be happening but it is. I wish I knew what to do about it. I don't. Soon it'll be all over and then. . . ."

Diane as always went right to the obvious. "Maybe we should give them something to eat," she interrupted.

He rolled the idea around in his mind, then dismissed it. But as it settled in he began to reconsider. Maybe that is exactly right. Maybe they were used to men giving them food. Even if they weren't hungry—and he gagged at the thought of why they were not. Maybe they smelled food in this house. And just maybe being fed would calm them. "How much food do you think there is here?"

"We came with the food boat. Plenty, I guess. Why?"

"Com'on," he said, rising from the table, "let's try something."

They began with the aging refrigerator, pulling out everything the dogs might find appetizing and piling it on the kitchen table. They went carefully through the cabinets. Diane dug into the small closets. "What about these?" she asked, holding up a tightly sealed jar. "There's about a dozen of them."

At first Larry was not even sure what the jars contained. Then he remembered his mother's annual fruit canning project. The smell of cooking fruit had filled the house for days, another country memory that had slipped from his city mind. "Try a few of them. Find something to dump them in. Who knows what they'll eat." Probably nothing, he thought, sickening. It was a waste of time, this whole thing. The plan could not possibly work, yet if there was the slightest chance, well, stranger things had happened, and it served at least one important purpose. It filled their time.

Diane washed out a blue plastic dish and emptied four jars into it. Their lids were tightly sealed, but she struggled and with some banging and hot water managed to get them open. Given a purpose, a chance to contribute, she showed herself to be an able and willing worker.

As they banged and tugged their way through the kitchen, the pack continued its racket. Even with the cotton in their ears it was a slow torture.

Josh walked into the kitchen, crying, "Make them stop, I don't wanna play this game." Larry took him back upstairs and showed both children how to cover only their ears with the fluffy pillows. Temporarily, at least, that satisfied them and he returned to work on the growing pile of food.

The making of a bizarre banquet covered the table. Piles of thawing meat, vegetables, cookies, bread, butter, ice cream, canned fruit, and even the contents of most of the cans of dog food they had brought to the island for Dopey. A heavy, almost pleasant aroma filled the room. "Anything else?" Larry asked.

"I wonder." Diane held up a small package. "This?" she asked. Larry could see the skull and crossbones on the red package. Rat poison!

He considered the idea briefly, then rejected it. "They might smell it and stay away from everything. It isn't worth the chance."

121

"Then how about some of my pills? The Valiums and the. . . ."

The pills again. Her answer for everything. "Okay," he said, hesitating then shrugging, "Yeah, why not? Let's try it." They put a few of the multicolored capsules aside for their own use, then set about mixing the tranquilizers. Diane opened the green and white plastic capsules and sprinkled their contents over the food. Larry emptied a large bottle of aspirin into a sheet of newspaper, folded the sheet carefully into fours, then smashed down with his hammer, disintegrating the tablets. At best, he decided, these drugs might calm the dogs down a little. Maybe even put them to sleep. At least shut them up. Anything.

Finally they were ready. Larry could not estimate the weight of the food, but it was most of what had been intended to last four adults, two children and one dog at least two weeks. Now, hopefully eleven dogs would devour it in one afternoon.

Outside, the nerve-racking chorus continued.

Diane settled down at the table. Cupping her hands to her forehead, she pulled at the long strands of her dark hair back. "How do we get it to them?" she asked tiredly.

Larry's head jerked up. "What?" The fact that she'd verbalized exactly what he himself was wondering startled him. It had been a long time since their thoughts had coincided.

She repeated the question.

He had no immediate answer. The front door and all the ground-floor windows were nailed shut, and he intended to leave them that way. The kitchen door was out, he was simply afraid to chance using it. And, with the dogs spread around the house as they were, a single pile of food would not be sufficient. Each of the dogs had to see the food as well as smell it. They had to be tempted by it. Then, hopefully, the temptation would be strong enough to overcome the strange power the shepherd held over them. That left. . . .

How do *we* give it to them, he wondered. We? That was actually funny. It had been a long time since he had thought of their relationship in terms of "we." About the only thing they still did together was attend dinner and cocktail parties. Maybe after all this, they could sit down and talk and. . . .

Later. He forced his mind back to the problem. Delivering the food. The ground floor was out. That left the second floor and the attic. Both would do, but both had inherent problems. If he chose to move from window to window on the second floor he would have to carry heavy piles of food to several different locations, and he wasn't sure he had enough energy for that. It also meant disturbing both the older women and the children.

We? How interesting. He smiled at the thought.

The attic would be more dangerous because he'd have to balance himself on the dormer window frame. One misstep and he'd be on the ground. It would also be difficult to get food to the few dogs directly behind the house. Still, the attic was the one site from which he could observe almost the whole pack. "I thought maybe I could throw it out from upstairs," he offered, and waited for her reaction. "From the attic."

"Will it work from there?" Nothing about the danger.

"Probably better than anyplace else."

She did not even hesitate. "Okay, then, let's get it up there."

Figuring it made more sense to move the heaviest stuff first, while she was least tired, Diane started with the meat. Cradling the pieces on a newspaper, she carried them to the stairs, nineteen steps by her own count, and handed them to Larry who took them upstairs. They worked silently, like two interlocking gears, the movement of one driving the second. It took twenty-five minutes to transport all the food to the second floor and pile it on six open sheets of newspaper.

Larry paused momentarily, and watched as Diane struggled with the accumulating weight of the food. With her hair pulled back and sweat on her forehead she looked more like a farmer's wife than a chic city-bred woman.

As Diane began moving the food eight steps across the hall to the bottom of the attic ladder, Larry pushed open the trapdoor onto his childhood. A wave of memories swept over him.

The temperature began dropping still further in the midafternoon, but the pack seemed oblivious to the cold. They howled at the house in a fury, as if the intensity of their howls could shatter the walls that protected the enemy. The pack instinct had taken over completely, the enemy of one becoming the enemy of all.

"It's dangerous up ahead," a state trooper in heavy-weather dress warned as he leaned into Kenny's four-wheel drive. "Roads still closed down. Plows are trying to work their way through, but it's tough moving. You best turn around and try it again in the morning." Kenny nodded agreeably and paid no attention. His mind was busy trying to figure out how to get around this horse's ass of a state trooper.

"Thanks, officer," he shouted as the trooper headed back to the warmth of his patrol car.

"Damn!" Len Hirschfeld said explosively. "I guess that's it, huh, Kenny?"

Kenny easily picked up the relief in Len's voice. "Guess so, Len," he answered. No, that isn't it at all, he thought. There was no way he was going to miss this opportunity to save Larry's ass once again. No way at all.

The situation at the house must really be desperate, Kenny figured, otherwise Larry would never have called. Now he would rub Larry's nose in his weakness. Now he would show him, prove to him, who the really successful brother was.

"Goddamn those troopers," Lenny exploded, "always giving orders. Pass me another Bud."

Kenny knew what dogs were capable of doing. War dogs tearing away barbed-wire barricades, sled dogs surviving the worst Alaskan storms, guard dogs brutally shredding invaders. If the dogs were determined enough, hungry enough, he decided, there was nothing Larry could do to stop them. He turned the Rover around and drove a couple of hundred yards down the road, around a bend and out of the trooper's sight.

Hungry enough. How much food is enough for a pack of dogs? Dogs had one eating peculiarity, he knew, one dog will eat enough to satiate itself, then stop. But as soon as another dog is present, the first dog will start eating again, deliberately gorging itself well beyond its own needs.

Without warning, he took a sharp right turn into a snow-covered field and opened up the engine.

"What the hell you doin'?" Len screamed as the bucking Rover caused half the can of beer to splash into his lap.

Kenny gunned the four-wheel through the snow, constantly shifting gears to keep the tires grabbing, and doing his best to make sure they didn't bog down in the soft drifts. "What's it look like I'm doing?" he screamed at the ashen-faced Hirschfeld. "I'm driving this thing to the dock, that's what the hell I'm doing!" He checked straight ahead then threw a hard glance across the front seat. "You think this is somethin', Len? This is nothin'! You shoulda seen the crap we drove through to reach Khe Sanh. The gooks threw everything at us. Now that," he screamed over the roar of the straining engine, "that was something."

How much food is enough? he wondered.

Len responded with a frightened half smile. "Oh."

"How you gonna know where you're going?" Pledge asked just loudly enough to be heard, the first words he'd spoken since they stopped at the roadblock. Pledge was a quiet person who rarely had much to say to anybody about anything. Thus when he did speak, people paid attention. What if he is quiet, Kenny had once defended him, that man can hunt the cat right out of a catfish.

"I'm going east, right. Can't miss the whole damn ocean. All we got to do is go far enough," Kenny shouted as they bumped and banged their way through what had once been a summer cornfield.

"You sure are one," Pledge said, laughing.

"One what?" Kenny wanted to know.

"I'm not exactly sure what it is"—Pledge chuckled—"but whatever it is, there's only one of them, and that's you!"

It was close enough to a compliment to be acceptable, so Kenny responded with a happy yell. He really liked being that one.

Then, when they were halfway through the field, peering through the windshield Kenny saw the first flake of new snow fall and stick. A few seconds later a second flake followed, and then the sky seemed to split open, releasing a blizzard. Kenny turned the heater to high, increased the speed of the Duco heavy-duty wipers and murmured a short silent prayer that the goddamn Rover wouldn't break down on him again.

The attic was dimly lit by the rays of late afternoon light which filtered through two dirty windows. Larry turned on the single unshaded light bulb and a dull, yellow light threw new shadows of dark and light that crisscrossed and filled the attic.

Larry stood three rungs down on the ladder and

peered into the small attic, remembering the hundreds of hours he'd spent playing in this space, another piece of his childhood tucked away. Once this attic had been full of old furniture and photograph albums and newspapers and shapeless piles of *Saturday Evening Posts,* and *Lifes* and *Looks* and *Colliers* and *Redbooks.* Sprawled across the musty piles of glossy paper, he had devoured the words and pictures. In this attic he had traveled to the most distant lands of the earth. He had been a fireman, a policeman, a cowboy and an Indian, a major leaguer, a soldier and even a writer. In this attic, he had been king.

That rubbish was gone now. A major cleaning job had wiped the place clean of most of the furniture and all the magazines. Fire hazards, of course. But the place still held that same friendly aroma. As his eyes slowly focused he made out the cobwebs in the corners. An old peg desk and a blackboard were pushed against a far wall. Somehow he didn't remember them. But across the room was the slatted bottom half of the bunk bed he'd once shared with Kenny. The top, the missing half, had been his by seniority. His parents had bought it for him as a gift, to help to make up for the pain he felt when they brought home another child. Standing on the ladder for one fleeting moment, he was again a fireman, policeman, cowboy and Indian. Then, as quickly as they had come, the memories were gone and the incessant barking of the pack filled his mind.

He climbed the final three steps of the ladder and, being careful not to step on the insulation, remembering he could fall through the ceiling if he did, walked across the creaking beams to the window. Looking down through the caked dirt, he could see a few of the dogs. They were on their feet, moving about jerkily, howling, straining forward yet not really advancing, as if held from the house by some invisible leash.

Larry gripped the window as firmly as he could and

tried to push it open, but the years had dried and expanded the wood and it was locked into the frame. He leaned forward carefully to see if the window and frame were in some way glued together. A thin dark line of separation between the two continued around the frame. They were not locked together, just stuck. He tried a second time, pushing up with his palms pressed against the top of the lower half of the window. Still, it would not budge. Angrily he slammed at the wood with his hammer, sending small splinters of wood and paint falling to the floor. But the shock of the blow tore the window loose from its frame and he managed to push it upward.

"Everything okay?" Diane yelled up to him.

"Yeah," he answered, breathing in the cold fresh air. Then he set to work.

First he laid a few timbers across the long, horizontal planks to form a platform for the food, then began a series of seemingly endless trips up and down the ladder. Until this point he had been careful not to think about his exhaustion, but it quickly became the most important consideration. He forced his mind to focus on a hot bath, or shower, or best of all, the feather mattress on the double bed in the front bedroom. And he forced himself to keep moving. It was ironic, he thought, but it was the constant howling of the dogs that kept him awake. If they quieted down he would be lulled to sleep, and then they could have the house. He would have laughed at the realization if only he wasn't so tired.

Only a few words passed between Larry and Diane as they worked. Larry didn't even realize all the food was up in the attic until Diane told him. He thrust his hands into the small of his back, pushing hard in an effort to relieve the dull ache that had settled there.

"That's it," she repeated, "everything's up there." Then she asked, her voice concerned, "Are you all right?"

"Just tired," he admitted.

Before making the final trip up the ladder he dunked his head under the cold water tap in the bathroom. "When I start heaving out the food," he explained to Diane, "you'll have to spot for me. I won't be able to see around to the sides of the house."

"Just tell me when," Diane replied crisply.

She watched Larry disappear into the attic, then returned to her post at the kitchen window. It was confusing, she thought, too many things happening at once, making it impossible to know which of the conflicting emotions she felt were real and which were false. And the strain, the unremitting strain! But she had to admit to herself that being part of something important gave her a good feeling inside.

It was freezing in the attic, but the cold served to revive Larry. The putrid smell rising from the soggy pile of food was beginning to nauseate him, so, without waiting any longer, he picked up a chunk of meat and leaned out the window to heave it, supporting himself by holding firmly to the wooden window frame with his left hand.

The first piece of meat soared through the air and landed with a whoosh less than three feet from the yelping wolfhound.

The surprised, frightened dog leaped up and away, temporarily quiet, then eyed the new hole in the snow curiously. Apparently suspecting danger, he did not move any closer to it.

Larry arched another hunk of meat to almost the same spot. The wolfhound backed away a little further, unable to comprehend the small explosions in the snow, yet reluctant to abandon his place in the tight circle. The dog looked to the nearby dogs for direction, but they continued the crazy chorus, stopping only when food began landing near them.

Again and again Larry threw, beginning to get the rhythm of the action. Bend down, pick up, lean forward, heave! All the dogs he could see were on their feet now, backing away from the holes in the snow.

His right arm began to ache from the throwing, but there was little he could do about it.

Heave. Heave. The food landed with a swoosh and disappeared into the snow. None of this was really possible, he knew. It was too absurd. He was a successful architect, a well-liked, intelligent, respected professional man. He could not really be leaning out a windowsill throwing chunks of meat down to a pack of murderous dogs, half scared out of his mind. It was just not possible.

But it was true. And those things down in the yard, those dogs, were ready to kill. They had killed. Those playful pets down in the yard. They had ripped into his father and torn the flesh from his bones.

Some of the dogs reacted immediately when the food landed, leaping into the air and moving away. Others dared to explore closer, but none of them even nibbled at the food.

Would the dogs accept this offering? Deciding he had tossed enough food to the dogs in front of the house Larry began to heave the food over his shoulder, aiming for the side of the house. "How am I doing?" he called down to Diane.

She had to leave the window to yell back up to him. "You're throwing it out too far from the house." He barely heard her answer. On his next throw he tried to cut down on his distance.

The shepherd had spotted him almost immediately. When Larry leaned on the icy windowsill a few stray bits of ice rolled down the shingles, hitting the metal gutters with a soft clang. The shepherd looked up at the man outlined against the white roof, perked its ears up, but made no other movement.

He could not comprehend what the man was doing. The shepherd waited until the enemy had finished his strange motions and only then did he rise up to investigate.

Larry watched the shepherd walk slowly through the pack. From time to time the dog would stop, sniff at some of the food, then move on. The pack's decision was his, Larry realized. If he ate, the rest of the pack would eat.

And if they did, then what?

The sky was dark and threatening again. Soon another snowfall would begin. *Diane is absolutely right,* he thought. *It is a Currier and Ives print. The white-topped forest trees, the flat open fields, the deep-brown snow-topped fence, the small bridge, the automobile sitting beyond the bridge, and even the frighteningly beautiful. . . .*

His mind abruptly shut out that thought. Instantly another popped up from his subconscious, the answer he had been seeking. The escape route from the house.

The answer had been sitting out there in the cold, right in front of him.

NINE

"My head hurts, Mommy," Marcy whined.

"I know, honey. My head hurts, too," Diane told her daughter.

"Why are they barking so much?" Josh demanded.

Diane sat on the edge of their bed doing her best to comfort and reassure her children. And trying to reassure herself. "They're animals," she tried to explain, knowing even as she spoke that was not an explanation, "and sometimes animals do things people can't understand." She had never been very good at explaining things to the children.

"Dopey doesn't," Marcy argued. The small dog was busy burrowing under the thick woven coverlet.

"That's because Dopey has people who love him and tell him what's right and wrong." This is stupid, she thought, all wrong. They don't understand what I'm talking about. "The dogs outside don't have anyone to love them, so they don't know when they're good and when they're bad." The dogs outside. That almost made her laugh. They weren't dogs at all. Dogs were docile things on leashes with carefully cut hair and fancy names. Pets to be loved. Expensive, prized possessions. Outside? Those vicious things? They were wild animals. They weren't dogs.

"Can't Daddy tell them?"

"He's trying, baby." And to her own surprise, she admitted that he was.

Josh sat up in bed, sending the gaily colored patchwork quilt flying. "Mommy, can't we go and help. . . ."

Marcy's pink face brightened. "Shh!" she ordered urgently. "Listen!"

They all listened. As suddenly, and seemingly as irrationally as the pack had begun its mad chorus, it ceased.

They sat rigid on the bed, listening intently, afraid to make even the slightest sound, afraid to risk shattering the magnificent silence.

Larry was sitting in the attic window watching the dusk ease in when the howling stopped. He had been sitting there for over an hour, trying to sketch the landscape in as much detail as possible. Occasionally, he had glanced down at the pack to see if they had made any move toward the food, but it remained untouched, and he had about given up hope they would accept it. The sudden silence startled him.

He racked his brain, trying to guess what strange need

kept them waiting in the yard? If not food, what? He dropped his pad and pencil into his lap and watched them, searching for the key that would unlock the mystery of their peculiar behavior.

The shepherd, he noticed, began moving as soon as the pack was quiet, circling the house. Larry watched him come around the nearest corner and lost sight of him as he turned the far one. Now what the hell is he doing?

As the shepherd completed its second trip around the house, Larry understood what was happening, if not why. For now, one by one, the other dogs were falling in behind the shepherd, and the growing chain of quiet dogs followed the leader around the house. The pack was regrouping.

He slammed the attic window shut and raced down into the kitchen. "What do you think?" Diane asked him from her post at the kitchen window.

"I don't," he told her. "Nothing they do makes any sense to me."

"Maybe they're leaving."

His mind seized on the possibility, only to reject it instantly. It would be too easy that way.

"Look," Diane said, pointing through the window. The dogs had stopped their circling and were now gathered in the front yard. They sat in a row before their leader. The shepherd waited until the dogs stopped shifting then trotted out in front of the pack. He dug his wedge-shaped muzzle into the snow and seized a chunk of meat in his mouth.

"He's taking it," Diane exclaimed, gripping Larry's arm and squeezing hard.

Moving a few steps away from the house, the shepherd dropped the meat. Then he stepped to the side and once more dug his snout into the snow. He picked up what looked to be part of a loaf of bread and dropped it near the meat. Three more times he buried his nose into the snow and emerged with food, until he had built a small pile in the yard. Then he turned and faced the pack, as if making sure he had their attention.

Deliberately the shepherd lifted its right hind leg and urinated on the food.

Diane gasped, then spewed out her hatred. "That disgusting, filthy animal."

The shepherd faced the house, emitted a piercing howl, then resumed his place in the line, legs out, ears erect, again patiently waiting.

"They're staying," Larry muttered dumbly. Diane relaxed her grip. He could feel the optimism that had carried her through the day evaporating.

"Why, Larry?" she asked in a bewildered voice. "What do they want?"

"Me," he said softly.

Diane laughed nervously. "What?"

"Me, Diane. I know it sounds absolutely insane, but those dogs want me." It was so clear to him now, so inevitable. It was no longer food the dogs were after. What they wanted, for some inexplicable reason, was him. That was their message in the violation of the food. Not enough, they meant, not nearly enough.

Diane did not understand and her voice rose as she challenged him. "What do you mean, Larry? Those animals out there, Larry, are stupid dogs. They don't think like that."

Explaining it to her was difficult because he did not fully understand it himself. But he knew. Absolutely. "The shepherd has made me its enemy. Maybe because of its mate, maybe for a dozen other reasons. But that dog is out there, waiting for me. And until I go out there. . . ." He left the sentence unfinished.

"That's not possible," Diane began, trying to convince

herself as well as her husband. "They're dogs. They don't have the brain—"

"The shepherd does." He said it curtly so as to leave no room for doubt, and the certainty in his voice confused her even more. Reality was no longer reality; the nightmare outside, the impossible, ugly nightmare, that was reality.

"Listen," she vaguely heard him say. "It'll be all right. We're safe in here. They can't get at us. . . ."

Two strong hands clamped down on her arms and a voice came from a great distance away. "Kenny's coming tomorrow. And I have a plan, Diane. I'm working on a plan!"

She was so tired. Tomorrow, she thought, we'll be home and everything will be all right. Tomorrow will be warm. And safe. She closed her eyes and collapsed into his arms, not hearing him at all.

"Goddamn no good horse manure sonofabitch bastard . . ."

"You're angry," Bob Pledge said dryly.

"Goddamn right I'm angry," Kenny agreed happily. "Goddamn night is here already and who the hell knows where we are?" They were half off a dirt road, caught in a snowbank with only a quarter of a tank of gas left.

Pledge looked over to Hirschfeld. "We're lost," he commented unnecessarily.

"So tell me something new," Hirschfeld responded. "Any beer left?"

The cold was beginning to seep into the cab, but Kenny did not feel it. His mind was too busy with his anger. The one goddamn time Larry broke down and actually asked him for help, and what happens? Caught in a snowbank who the hell knows where is what happens. Goddamn Larry is always so goddamn right. Irresponsible. Can't take care of himself. The man is goddamn right.

He gunned the engine again. The heavy snowtires clawed at the snow-covered earth, slid, gripped again. Shifting quickly into reverse, Kenny began trying to rock the Rover free. Back-shift-forward-shift-back-shift-forward. He'd been there! Vietnam! The United States friggin' Marine Corps! Yeah, what would have happened to Larry if they blew those mortars at him? Let's see him run his mouth about responsibility then! Goddamn hero, that's what he was over there, goddamn motherloving hero.

"Rock-a-bye baby on the treetops," Hirschfeld sang loudly.

"Shut up," Kenny ordered. . . . Shift-back-shift-forward. . . . The Rover suddenly jerked free, snapping their heads backward, and they were off again. Kenny leaned forward in the driver's seat, as if trying to push the Rover faster. He wasn't going to blow it this time. Goddamn it! No way. He couldn't—he was a hero, and he had the medals to prove it.

The answer was the old Chevy coupe. Once he reached that, Larry knew, there was nothing the dogs could do to prevent him from escaping. The car itself was a weapon. The only problem was reaching it. He stared at the rough sketch he'd drawn. A square represented the house. A series of small x's were the dogs. Two short parallel lines indicated the bridge and a small rectangle was the car. Other wavy lines represented the contour of the land. Although it was difficult, if not impossible, to figure the lay of the land when it was covered with snow, he had decided that any estimate was better than nothing. And a long time ago he'd learned to include every variable in his plans. The completed sketch resembled a gameboard. The object of the game was simply to get six players from the square to the rectangle before the x's could tear them apart.

Night had arrived in the brief moments it had taken him to carry the unprotesting Diane upstairs. "Mommy's very tired," he had explained to the children as he placed her on their bed, "so you guys watch over her."

"When we gonna eat, Dad?" Josh whispered conspiratorially.

Diane lay still, her breathing heavy but regular. It had been a rough day for her, he knew, much rougher than he would have believed she could handle. And she'd done well. Better than well, very well. She'd helped. "Sleep first," he whispered back to his son.

Corny had fallen asleep on the floor, and Larry carefully covered her with a blanket. But his mother was awake, the effect of the pills having worn off. "Hi, Mom," he said softly, sitting down next to her.

She smiled at him without lifting her head from the pillow.

"How you feeling?" he asked.

Frieda closed her eyes and answered calmly. "I'm all right." This was their first private moment together since. . . . It seemed like forever. "Was it horrible?" Tears came to her eyes.

"It all happened so quick," he told her in the same soft voice. "The dogs were there, and he wanted to fight them."

She buried her head in the pillow and sobbed.

Larry gently rubbed her shoulders and neck. "He wouldn't let them beat him, Ma," he whispered. "He just wouldn't give up." He wanted to cry, needed to cry, but not now. Later, he promised, later. Kissing her on the back of her neck and squeezing her hand tightly, he left her sobbing quietly. She would disturb no one, as was her way.

Larry counted nine chimes as the clock on the mantel signaled the hour. Nine? It didn't seem possible. Could it actually have been three hours ago? He had no idea how long he'd been sitting in the easy chair studying the sketch, but it certainly didn't seem that long.

Larry turned his attention to the wrinkled sketch.

It intrigued and yet baffled him. The answer was there, on that piece of paper. It was there, he just had to find it. How to get by the dogs to the safety of the car? There was no way the trip could be made on the ground.

His eyes shut. He forced them open. He could not sleep.

A tunnel? Ridiculous. What difference did it all make anyway? None of these plans were necessary. Kenny would arrive in the morning, drive the pack back into the woods. Larry realized how badly he wanted to believe that.

But Kenny. . . . Larry knew him so well, and just in case something went wrong this time, there had to be an alternate plan. Anytime Kenny was involved, there had to be an alternate plan.

Accepting that, he worked into the night. The lack of sleep was beginning to tell, exaggerating the aches and pains of the last two days, making it impossible for him to concentrate for any length of time. The easy chair was too comfortable, he realized, so he moved to the harder kitchen chair.

The answer was obvious. He knew it. Then why couldn't he see it? Again he went through their options, cutting them down one by one. They could not go through the pack. They could not go under the pack. And they could not go around the pack. Therefore, he had to go over them. It was so simple. Then he would drive the car up flush against the house, open a door, and carry his family away to safety.

The square that was the house on his sketch pad slowly faded into the x's, and for a minute the x's were inside the square: the dogs were in the house! The significance of that jerked him awake, and set him to concentrating on his problem once again.

Over the pack. He drew a straight line from the kitchen door to the car. No, not the kitchen door. It wasn't high enough. From the attic window. He erased his first line and drew another, this time from roughly where the attic window was to the rectangle. That would have to be the escape route. But how?

The more he stared at it, the more the straight line on the sketch looked familiar. Like it belonged. Like he had seen it before on a thousand other sketches and plans and blueprints. Of course he'd seen it before. He'd seen it on every blueprint of every private house he'd worked on. The telephone wire. The single strand of strong weather-resistant wire that connected each individual house to the rest of the world. The lifeline. And then he understood why everything suddenly became clear on the roof. The wire had been the giveaway. The long, sagging black wire stretched from the house to a wooden terminal pole far beyond the gorge. His eyes had unconsciously followed its line, straight as an arrow, but instead of following it all the way to the pole, he'd stopped as it passed over the car. It had been the wire that caught his attention, not the car, and he just hadn't been smart enough to see it. The goddamn telephone wire! Goddamn Alexander Graham Bell! He had his escape route. Over them.

At first light tomorrow morning he would climb back into the attic and determine just how strong the wire was. It had to be strong enough to support his weight. As soon as he was sure the wire would hold him.

He forced himself to slow down. What the hell was going on? Where were his brains? None of this superman stuff was going to be necessary. Kenny would arrive in the morning. Sometime in the morning, or by early afternoon at the latest, but he *would* be there. And they could easily hold out until then. There was no rush to risk his life with some damn fool high-wire act. He could just relax until Kenny came, not worry, relax. . . .

Heavy eyelids closed over his eyes; he was fading into unconsciousness. He forced himself to wake.

Must not sleep! He flooded his mind with dire warnings, but even so he could barely manage to keep his eyes open. The lids were so heavy, and sleep seemed warm, safe. "I will not sleep," he said aloud.

This time he got up and went to the sink. Cold water on his face helped.

The water dripped onto his clothes and the floor as he went to the window and peered out into the yard. They were still there. The reflection of the kitchen light burned off the shepherd's blazing green eyes. Don't *they* ever sleep!

He decided to do a few brief jumping exercises to get his blood circulating. Up-in-the-air-two-three-four. The stretching emphasized every ache. Could they see him from out there? Up-two-three-four. After finishing a dozen leaps he had to stop to catch his breath. *Dogs,* he thought. "Dogs," he said loudly. "Dog tag." Then, "dog-face." "Dogcatcher. Doggone." Good one. "Doggone," he repeated. "Dogtired. Dogleg. Doghouse." He was fully awake again. "Dog days. Dog-eared. Dog-eat-dog. Dog paddle. Dogwood. Dagwood." No, Dagwood definitely did not count. "Dogwood. Dogmatic. Dogtired." Was that a repeat? Hard to remember. "Dog. . . ." They began to come slower now. "Dogshit. Dog town. Dog run." His mind was running down. "Dog . . . track. Dog . . . it." Seating himself at the kitchen table, he pictured each word in his mind. The three letters, d, o, and g. Dog, it was a silly word to describe a silly animal. "Doggie bag," he remembered, and "Doggiedo." This time nothing could keep him awake. He fell asleep leaning on his elbows on the kitchen table.

He was entering a carnival funhouse with a younger Diane. They burst through two tall wooden doors into the dark, riding in the front seat of a red car with gold scrolls twisting on its sides. A laughing witch leaned forward and cackled at them, but the lantern she held lit their way out of her chamber into a cave, where they barely avoided a rockfall. Just as they were about to be squashed by a mammoth boulder the red cart made a sharp right turn and they were trapped inside an animal cage, looking out through the bars at the pointing, laughing spectators. Another quick turn and they were dropping through darkness. Diane gave a short shriek and her long hair streamed out behind her with the unexpected drop. Larry thought he was laughing.

They slowed, almost stopped, in the pitch black. Unexpectedly, thin strands of webbing ran through their hair, tickling them with terror, and they screamed. And then laughed. The car speeded up and started climbing, the wheels clicking over the track as the cart rose higher. And higher.

Then dropped them into a pirates' den, where they were being treated to a public hanging. A one-eyed buccaneer screamed and swung his cutlass at them. But they were gone around another corner and into another adventure. Up ahead was still another door and in the dark Larry could not see exactly what it was. As they rolled closer he realized they were approaching the giant, constantly opening and closing jaws of a bulldog. Huge, bright eyes glared at them. Two sparkling, sharp bloody incisors bid them welcome. Larry thrust his weight against the front of the car, trying to make it stop. Not into the jaws, he pleaded. But the car rolled closer and closer. The eyes grew even bigger. The jaws closed firmly, and opened again, waiting. And finally they rode over the huge teeth into the mouth of the dog. The fearsome jaws clamped shut behind them. He saw nothing.

A hand was on his shoulder, gently shaking him. "Larry," a distant voice urged in a whisper. "Wake up! Larry. You have to come upstairs. There's a dog upstairs."

He shoved his knuckles into his eyes to clear his vision. Corny Cornwall was leaning over him. A dream? No, her body gradually came into focus. "What, Corny?" he asked irritably. He had fallen asleep, dammit, he'd been asleep.

"There's a dog upstairs. You have to come upstairs and get rid of the dog. It's not supposed to be in the house."

Larry breathed deeply, trying to shake the cobwebs from his mind. "Okay, Corny," he replied gently, "show me where the dog is." How could he have fallen asleep? How long? At least an hour, he guessed. Possibly even more.

They walked upstairs together, Larry staying a step behind to support the old woman. Halfway to the top the clock began to chime, announcing three A.M. He'd slept another three hours. It didn't seem possible. The sun would be rising soon and then he would have to start working. Working? The plan, he suddenly remembered. The details were loose in his mind, he'd have to check his notes.

At the top of the stairs Corny turned and walked toward her room. The door had been left open. Larry stepped onto the landing and started to follow. "Where's the dog, Corny?" he asked.

"I locked it in the bathroom," she told him. "It came in the hall window and went into the bathroom, so I closed the door behind it."

"Good going." He smiled at her. It was cold in the hall, he noticed, much colder than downstairs. He'd have to close the window. The bathroom door was indeed closed. As he started to open it, Larry paused and looked toward Corny. "It's okay," he whispered loudly, smiling, then opened the bathroom door. The golden retriever hit him chest high.

The surprise, as much as the impact, sent him crashing backward against the far wall. He fell hard, arms and legs flailing. The retriever was on him even as he fell, pressing the attack, tearing at him, ripping savagely at any exposed part of his body, trying for his face.

Diane appeared at her door almost at once. This time she did not retreat, this time, without pausing, she went after the dog. She grabbed at its flank, trying to pull it off, but the dog's strength made it impossible for her to move it.

Larry instinctively coiled himself up as best he could, desperately trying to protect his body. He kicked out at the dog, hard unaimed thrusts, until finally one of his desperate kicks hit the dog in the chest, pushing her a few feet off him. But he had no time to recover before she was at him again, an incredible sixty-two-pound bundle of violence, her teeth seeking a deadly hold.

Her claws scraped across his face, shredding the surface of the skin.

Somehow Larry managed to throw the dog off once again. But the frenzy of the animal's attack had drained him. He slumped exhaustedly against the wall, peering stupidly as the snarling animal crouched before him, readying itself to spring again.

Diane raced back into the children's room, searching for a weapon. Anything, anything would do.

There was nothing. The snarling sounds from the hallway prodded her on. Desperately, she grabbed at the slender white base of a bottle lamp, ripping the cord from its socket. The shade dropped off as she ran back into the hall.

Diane looked for a chance to hit the dog, but the retriever moved too quickly, leaving no opening, no vulnerable spot.

The retriever had gained a hold on Larry's thigh and held on tightly, her razor teeth sunk into his flesh. Screaming wildly, Larry reached down with his hands to try to tear her from his bleeding leg.

In doing so, he left his neck exposed. The dog released her hold on his leg and started for his throat just as five-year-old Josh came running out of his room.

The boy came at the dog from her blind side and shoved her. Automatically the dog turned and snapped at her new foe without looking, catching his forearm and biting deeply.

But then something happened. The golden retriever, looking at the boy, changed almost instantly. For that moment she was no longer the same vicious dog, as if the sight of the child had caused her to remember something long forgotten. She stood motionless for another second and Diane crashed the lamp down across the side of her skull, killing her instantly.

Larry lay doubled up on the floor, aware of pain and an overwhelming anger. He had been beaten. The dog had overcome his most potent weapon, his human intelligence, rendering him vulnerable. The retriever had penetrated his walls. He had left a single opening, an upstairs hall window, and the dog had discovered it and launched her attack. Physically, she had won. He was alive only because her heritage had betrayed her at the last minute. Her victory had been greater than that, though. His leg hurt, but the worst pain was the knowledge that he was less than he had believed. His father had died when he had left him behind, when he had run. And now his wife had had to act to save his life. The dogs; the rotten, disgusting dogs, had humiliated him, made him less of a man.

Diane leaned over him. "How do you feel?" she asked. Somehow she had ministered to the children and calmed the older women.

Larry could not look at her. "Okay," he grunted, "it's all right." The body of the retriever lay a few feet from him, the brown-gold hair matted with blood.

Diane ripped up his trouser leg to inspect his wound, but Larry was only half aware of her actions. He found it difficult to take his eyes from the body of the dog.

"Do you think it was rabid? It bit Josh too, right through his skin," Diane told him.

In death the dog was almost beautiful. Rabid? "Wash the wound out carefully," he said. What did he know of rabies? Shots? He vaguely knew about them. Dozens of them, over a long period, painful injections into the liver. Suddenly he remembered. "We have to cut the dog's head off."

If she reacted at all he was not aware of it. "Why?"

The clarity of his thoughts surprised him. "We have to bring it back with us. They can tell about rabies."

"Can you stand?"

Together they went to the kitchen where she washed out his wounds and wrapped his thigh tightly. The pain was constant, but bearable. Another debt, he knew, that would have to be paid.

The shepherd had picked up the sounds of the struggle. The dog listened, understood and was not surprised when the battle ended without a canine howl of victory. It had been a successful probe. The enemy's citadel had been breached. And the enemy was tiring.

It would be the enemy himself who would provide the final opening. Until then the pack would follow as he led. But in the end, he knew that he would triumph, that he would kill this enemy.

TEN

The skin at the bottom of the dog's neck sliced easily. Larry had laid the retriever's body on the kitchen counter, its head and neck over the sink. He cut carefully through the flesh, aiming at what he guessed to be the shoulder bone, pushing harder on the knife when it was necessary to cut through the tendons and muscles.

As he made his first cut, Larry discovered a worn leather collar. He sliced it away, wondering about the people who had fastened it there, who had owned this dog, trained it, and then left it on the island to die. In death, the beast had once again become a pet. He threw the collar on the floor near an open garbage bag.

The cut itself was clean and little blood dripped into the basin. Larry was bothered only when the head dropped backwards and the brown eyes opened in a death stare.

Diane spent the rest of the night between the two floors, ministering to whomever seemed to need it most. First the children, then Larry, then the children again, finally the women. The retriever's teeth had left a number of small punctures in Josh's forearm. They did not bleed badly, but the child's arm was swollen and the area around the bite had begun turning a sickly yellow-brown, which worried her greatly. Josh, however, seemed to take everything in stride, and once Diane had carefully cleaned and bandaged his arm, he ceased crying.

Larry, she noticed, had become strangely quiet, but he seemed full of energy. Assuming this to be an aftermath of the fight, she gave it little thought. The sun would be up in a few hours and the ordeal would soon be over. Larry would be fine, his wounds were clean and not as deep as Josh's, so it was the psychological effect of the pack on the children that most worried her. She had already decided to consult a child psychiatrist in the city, and count on him to ensure that the horrors of the past days would not leave a permanent scar. Hopefully, the children would survive the ordeal, learn from it, and maybe even be toughened by it. But, God, hopefully they would not be scarred.

Larry discovered that by grabbing hold of the muzzle and lifting the head upward, he could cut through the neck more easily. He felt no compassion for the dog. It had attacked and tried to kill him and in turn had been killed. His single regret was that it was not the shepherd he was decapitating. That truculent gray hulk who sat so unreachable in the snow. He cut upwards, making a jagged line toward the ear. It had been stupid luck, that's all. There was no way the pack could have known that the hall window was open. The retriever had obviously jumped up on the rear garbage pile, leaped from there to the porch roof and finally from the porch through the open window. They could not have known. He cut again, across the back of the neck now, leaving the head hanging by little more than a sliver of skin. The tongue lolled grotesquely. The shepherd certainly wasn't stupid, in fact, it was an unusually bright animal. But smart enough to spot an open window and understand that it was a passageway into the house? No way. It was luck. Silly, stupid, outright, old-fashioned dumb luck.

The retriever had come only for him. There could be no question about that. It must have seen Corny, or sensed her, when she went to close the bathroom door. But it hadn't attacked her; it had waited for him. Somehow, in some incredible, mystical way the shepherd had communicated its hatred of Larry to the retriever.

The dog had waited for him! There had to be some

rational explanation, and he decided he would consult an expert as soon as they were back home.

Gingerly, Larry picked the severed head of the retriever up out of the sink and dropped it into a plastic bag. After twisting the bag closed, he placed it inside a brown garbage bag and stored it in the refrigerator. It probably made no difference where it was kept, but Larry didn't know for sure, and it couldn't possibly hurt to keep the thing fresh.

At first he thought disposing of the body might prove troublesome, but he quickly found a solution. He would use it to make a point. He would communicate his own hatred to the shepherd. Larry was beginning to look forward to the inevitable confrontation with the shepherd. He was smiling grimly as he returned to the attic.

The sun never appeared on the mainland that morning. Instead, the overhanging dark storm clouds lightened somewhat and it was morning. The Rover pulled onto the dock just before full light, and its three passengers stepped out into the light snowfall.

Their attention was immediately captured by the angry waters of the Sound. It was close to high tide, and four-foot waves smashed into the pilings, sending great sprays of mist shooting into the air. The few fishing boats moored in the cove bobbed high on the water and then, as if the world below them had suddenly vanished, collapsed, slamming down into the water. "Jesus H. Christ," Len Hirschfeld said thickly, "look at that goddamn water jump."

Kenny shifted his feet uneasily. "It's not exactly sailing weather," he agreed.

"We can't go out in this," Hirschfeld said authoritatively.

Kenny paid no attention. Having been brought up on the island, he was an experienced boatman. The water was rougher than he had thought it would be, but certainly that didn't make a crossing impossible. Once they found a good boat they could swing north of Orient Point, staying close to the shore, hugging the beach. . . .

First things first. Get a good boat. "Let's just see what happens," he replied noncommittally.

They walked through the heavy mist that hung over the dock to Tony's Fishnet, a small aluminum and plastic luncheonette. A large net hung from the ceiling along with two life preservers, one from the *Maria Elgarant,* and the other from the *Miss Meredith*. In one corner a group of winter fishermen who had hoped to go out for the day were huddled over a tarnished silver coffee pot. Kenny went over to them.

He stood silently next to their table for a few minutes, waiting for them to acknowledge his presence. But the attention of the group focused on a wind-burned man whose face was so covered with wrinkles that Kenny was reminded of a Venetian blind. The aged fisherman was unreeling a long rambling story about a Long Island lobster fisherman who had tried to computerize his boat.

Kenny saw no point to the story but listened nonetheless, laughing at what he judged to be the right time. He knew the fishermen were aware of him, but there was a protocol to be observed, so he stood waiting patiently.

Finally the storyteller finished, drew a big laugh, leaned back, drowned the remnants of his coffee, and acknowledged Kenny. "Son?"

"I've got a problem," Kenny said forthrightly. "I need to get across to Burrows Island."

"You sure do got a problem," one of the younger fishermen commented loudly, looking around in expectation of laughter.

"I'll pay," Kenny offered.

The storyteller took a deep breath, as if to ensure that he would have enough air to complete a lengthy statement, but actually only to guarantee he held everyone's attention. "Son," he said quietly, "can you pay for a new fish boat? 'Cause that's what it might cost you. The channel's real shallow out by that island, much too shallow for the draft on most of our boats, and we got a real good blow working out there today. That's why we ain't out there right now. And there ain't nobody around here who wants to be in or even near low water when that wind is pushing boats around."

"I've got to get there," Kenny continued, "I'll pay a lot."

The storyteller gave Kenny a look that asked if he had been paying any attention at all to the answer he'd already received. "Good luck to you, son," he told him, then swung his body around and dove back into the middle of another conversation.

Kenny understood he had been dismissed. But as he joined Pledge and Hirschfeld across the small room he lied confidently, "They're gonna think about it." Behind him the storyteller leaned forward and said something that drew a great uproar of laughter.

A steady thump-thump from the staircase brought Frieda Hardman to the door of her room. She opened it only enough to see what was making the strange noise in the hallway. Larry, she saw, was climbing up the stairs backward, dragging something heavy after him. She couldn't see what it was, even after she opened the door a bit more. Reaching the top of the stairs, Larry rested briefly, then resumed dragging his strange load down the hall.

It turned out to be a large white bedsheet with something wrapped inside. Larry held the four corners of the sheet as he dragged it down the hall. As he went by—she closed the door briefly because she didn't want him to think she was spying—Frieda caught a glimpse of what looked like the body of a brown dog wrapped in the sheet.

She knew immediately it was the dog that had attacked her son in the hallway.

After he passed she moved to the other side of the door and peered through the crack between the hinges. Larry looked so tired, so used. A stain discolored the bottom of the sheet, and although it appeared to be brown, she knew it was blood. At the base of the ladder leading up to the attic, Larry hefted the bag up over his right shoulder. Slowly he climbed up the ladder, pulling the sheet and its grisly contents up with him into the attic.

The only thing in the whole wide snow-covered world that Sergeant Stewart Stromfeld wanted was some sleep. The few hours he'd managed to catch on the lumpy cot stuffed into a rear cell had done little more than whet his appetite for more of the same. He'd been stuck in the station since the storm first hit, surviving on the cold roast beef sandwiches Jerry brought over from next door, trying to make less than half the normal force cover emergencies the entire force would have been pressed to handle adequately. In the last twenty-four hours he'd had two reported missing children, a birth in a stuck car, one bowling-alley roof collapse, a Cadillac slide into the living room of a nice middle-class family, and the discovery of three-foot-long footprints at the end of Maple Street in Port Jefferson accompanied by the reported sighting of a man "about ten feet tall, completely covered with hair, walking upright, who ran when spotted by the five-foot-six-inch-tall white-haired town librarian." And then there had been the people out on Burrows Island who were calling again to ask the police to save them from a pack of wild dogs. Stromfeld wanted to suggest that they tell it to the ASPCA, but he knew Captain Kelly would not appreciate his attempt at humor. "Look," he told the caller, "I'd like to send someone over there to help you, but this storm is getting worse. It's snowing again here and we're supposed to get another four inches this afternoon. We're bleeding for help here." He caught himself. As a professional man he was not supposed to complain to civilians. "I'll do my best to get somebody out there first thing tomorrow," he promised politely. "As soon as we have the men we're gonna make a sweep of all the outer islands. We'll stop on Burrows first, I promise you that."

"What about the Coast Guard?" the voice on the phone demanded.

"No chance. They just lost a small cutter picking up survivors of the Greek wreck. They're out there now trying to find the crew. They're only answering emergency calls, and if it's not an emergency you gotta wait your turn."

"But it is an emergency," the voice complained.

"You still gotta wait your turn."

There was a reluctant silence on the other end of the phone. Com'on, Sergeant Stromfeld said silently, I can't stay on this thing all day. "Sergeant," the voice finally crackled into his ear, "do you know what the incubation period for rabies is?"

Rabies? "Listen, I wouldn't worry about that. There hasn't been a reported case on the island since—"

"Do you know?" the voice persisted.

"Not exactly. I'd say get to the doctor as soon as possible." How was he supposed to know that? He was a cop, not a doctor.

The person on the other end of the phone sighed deeply. "Thank you, officer." After a slight pause, she concluded, "If there's any chance you can get here sooner. . . ."

"Then we will," he finished the thought. "We know where you are."

After hanging up, Sergeant Stromfeld set about pecking out his report on the Remington. On a believability scale, he decided he had more faith in the pack of wild dogs than in the ten-foot-tall monster.

Diane cradled the phone, then stood silent, listening to her husband moving about in the attic.

He was no longer tired. In fact, he felt alert and well rested. The cold air felt marvelous on his face as he leaned out the attic window and watched the pack. The dogs were quiet, merely shifting position occasionally. They can't be too damn comfortable out there, he thought. Too bad. Too, too bad.

Larry felt confident enough to stand up on the window-sill. The steady, slight breeze sent his shirt billowing out and his pants ballooned, but he liked the macho, captain-of-the-ship feeling it gave him. Standing up also provided a much better view of the area. As he remembered, the telephone wire passed directly over the roof of the car. In fact, the midpoint of the wire, the spot where it sagged closest to the ground, looked to be almost precisely over the car. The drop from the wire to the snow-covered roof appeared to be no more than five or six feet.

By leaning slightly forward he could see that the wire was attached to a terminal at the corner of the roof, maybe eighteen feet above the ground. Somehow he would have to check the strength of the connection. If it wasn't strong enough to hold his weight he would have to figure a way to strengthen it. The other end of the wire, the connection to the distant pole could not be tested.

His pain had disappeared in his excitement. Seemingly hours ago Diane had bound his thigh and washed out the scratches across his face. The only really bothersome relic of the fight was a slight scratch on his eyelid that caused him to blink periodically, but he'd gotten used to that.

Directly below him the ground was littered with the food the pack had rejected. The smaller pieces pocked the snow as far around the house as he could see. From above, the multicolored blotches against the snow made the yard resemble an artist's palate. Near the kitchen door a mound of blowing snow covered the remains of the Airedale. Across the gorge a second snow mound hid the shattered body of the small shepherd. Neither body had been disturbed by the hungry dogs.

Larry had decided to try to distract the dogs with the body of the third dog he'd killed, the retriever, and then inspect the telephone wire connection while they were busy with it.

Climbing back into the attic, he seized the body of the dog by its front legs, being careful not to touch it near the severed neck, and rested it on the windowsill. The body emitted a strange odor, a combination of caked blood and musty fur.

Lifting it as high as he could, he heaved it from the window. It didn't quite clear the edge of the roof, and one of its legs caught in the gutter and snapped sharply, causing the body to twist end over end as it slammed into the snow with a loud thump.

Larry smiled.

For the first time since they had laid siege to the house, the dogs broke rank, congregating around the headless body, circling it, smelling it, a few even touching it with their muzzles. From the random whines and occasional barks, Larry knew that he had hurt them. Paying back a bit more of his debt. But it was only the beginning. He would show them. This battle was not man against dog, he told himself, but human intelligence versus animal intelligence. Thus they had no real chance against his trained, and now acutely alive, mind.

Leaving the pack gathered about the body of the retriever, Larry climbed back onto the windowsill and got ready to move out on the roof. Facing back into the attic, he squatted, then cautiously rested both knees on the sill. Moving gradually, digging his fingernails into the wood frame, he set his right foot into the snow. It slid. He brought it back up and tried again, this time pushing the toe of his foot firmly into the roof. Again it slipped.

Carefully crawling back into the attic, he removed his shoes and socks and rolled up the bottom of his pants. Then he again climbed out onto the roof. He could feel his toes gripping the rough shingles beneath the snow. His bare feet provided much better traction than leather soles, and he found he could control the skidding. His feet hurt. His feet felt wonderful.

Little by little he levered his body out the window until he was flat on his stomach against the roof, his hands still gripping the windowsill. The incline was not quite as sharp as he had figured it would be, no more than thirty degrees, certainly less than the pointed tops of the suburban boxes he'd designed. Once he was sure there was little danger of his sliding, he began to move around on the roof, inches at a time, to get used to the footing. With each movement a small ball of snow cascaded from the roof, but that did not bother him. In fact, the newly bared spots would provide better traction for his return.

Carefully, he pulled his body sideways toward the right side of the dormer, the side nearest the yard, keeping a firm grip on the sill. He cautiously released his right hand from the sill and dug down through the snow to the shingles, trying to figure a way to get a firm grip. At best, the overlapping front edge of the shingle offered a tenuous hold. Taking the hammer from his belt, he wedged the sharp nail-pulling claw under the front of one shingle and lifted. The shingle moaned and tore partially loose from the roof, allowing him to slide his fingers underneath and hold the shingle, giving him a much more secure grip. Now he knew how he would pull himself to the terminal.

Reaching out as far as he could, still without releasing his left-hand hold on the windowsill, Larry worked a second shingle loose. Then, resting the hammer between his chest and the roof, he grasped the second shingle with his right hand. He tugged at it as best he could, testing its ability to hold him, and when he was confident it would, loosened his left hand ever so slightly, holding it inches above the windowsill, ready to grab hold instantly. Now he was out on the roof. And scared. For one moment, he did not breathe.

He inhaled slowly, but did not slide. Then he very deliberately slid the fingers of his left hand underneath the first shingle, scratching the back of his hand against the roof itself, and gripped it tightly between his thumb and the rest of his hand. Secure in the knowledge that the shingles would support his weight, he began moving across the roof.

Each movement was exhausting and painful. The cold bit into him. The slight breeze blew fresh snow into his face, irritating his scratched eye, and the rough edges of the exposed shingles grated against his skin, rubbing it raw. But slowly he continued to work his way across the roof, loosening one shingle with the hammer claw, grasping it in his right hand, and once confident it was secure, moving his left hand to the shingle last vacated by his right hand.

The distance to be covered was about fifteen feet, and when he was halfway he relaxed momentarily and held his spot on the roof. For a fleeting instant he wondered if Diane would discover him out on the roof. He was not sure if he wanted her to or not. Below, he saw, the dogs had lost interest in the body of the retriever, although a few of them kicked at the snow, almost as if they were trying to cover the corpse.

Then he started moving again in the same, slow, aggravating fashion. Loosen, stretch, grasp, change hands.

In this slow way he made it across the expanse of roof to the telephone wire terminal. When he reached the edge of the roof overlooking the yard he gently let his feet slide down into the tin gutter. Before putting any weight on it, he tested it carefully, and discovered, if he did not push against it, the gutter would support him. Then, methodically, he turned his body on the roof and began examining the connection.

Frieda Hardman walked into the kitchen, interrupting Diane in the middle of a lonely thought about the safety of her New York apartment. "I'm sorry, Diane," she started, slightly embarrassed, feeling like an interloper in her own kitchen, "but I just couldn't stand it in that room anymore."

"No, no, no," Diane said, "sit down, please sit down." She noticed her mother-in-law had finally taken off the awful flowered dress she had worn at dinner, and replaced it with another equally awful house dress. And, she thought, how strange that her mind should notice something so utterly unimportant. "There's some coffee on the stove. Larry made it."

Frieda waved the thought away. "No, thank you. I'm okay."

There were heavy shadows under her eyes, suitcases Larry would call them. She'd been crying. Something had to be said, Diane thought. "Mrs. Hardman," she began. How strange, how terribly formal that sounded. "I'm so sorry. I just. . . ." She waved a hand in the air, having no idea how to continue.

"I know you are," Frieda told her, trying to raise a smile. "I know how terrible this is for. . . ." She suppressed a sob, took a deep breath, then continued, "I know this is a terrible thing. And. . . ."

"For all of us." It would have made things easier if

she could have moved around the table and put her arms around the older woman. But Diane could not bring herself to do it. Attempting to maintain some sort of conversation, anything at all, she plunged on. "This is like a gothic novel. People trapped in a house. Something frightening . . . terrifying outside. Only of course it's not a book. It's actually happening to us."

A cigarette would have tasted wonderful at that moment. A cigarette? Some good grass! She had neither. Cigarettes were unhealthy and stained her fingers yellow, and she only smoked marijuana with friends, away from the apartment. Larry would not permit it in the apartment.

"What's going to happen?"

"Kenny is supposed to be on his way."

"Kenny," the older woman said softly, as if speaking of a small child, "Kenny."

"Why don't they get along?"

Frieda knew a question had been addressed to her. "Excuse me?"

"Larry and Kenny, why don't they get along with each other?"

She considered that. Why did her two sons not get along? Why weren't they friends? For so many reasons, she thought. They were so different. Kenny had always been independent while Larry was a dependent child. Kenny was so physical, a brave adventurer, Larry was an early reader, drawn to books. Larry hated having to call on his younger brother for help, Kenny resented being compared to his older brother in school. Larry was dependable, Kenny was less reliable, she decided. They had always been different, and resentment, maybe even hatred grew from those differences. But she had never been able to change them. "They've always been different," was all she said, making it clear she did not want to discuss it.

Diane stared at her own slender white fingers. Somewhere, sometime, one of her long fingernails had cracked and a second had actually broken. The broken nail had a jagged edge, like one of those microscopic close-ups of used razor blades in television commercials, she thought incongruously, and smiled. It would have to be filed, sanded, reconstructed. When they got back. When she had time for it. Perhaps.

"Are we really trapped in this house?" Frieda asked.

"Right now we are. The dogs won't. . . ." Diane stopped talking as she realized her mother-in-law wasn't listening to her.

Frieda Hardman was lost in her thoughts at the kitchen window. She looked out upon them, dogs grazing in a field of snow. Thomas had loved dogs. They understood thoughts, he used to say, they're smart, they know what a man is thinking.

Go away, she thought, go away and leave us alone. But she did not move from the window, and the pack did not stir.

The telephone wire was constructed of surprisingly heavy cable, rubber encased, and securely fastened to a series of metal connections. Although there was no way of accurately figuring how much weight it would support before tearing loose or snapping in half, Larry was confident it would support him. It was simple physics: The connections had to be secure enough, and the wire itself strong enough to support its own weight. In most American housing developments that was negligible, because the houses were huddled together and telephone poles were close by. But it was different in the country. There, great lengths of wire were needed to connect houses which were normally set well back from roads and telephone poles. A single expanse of wire might stretch for more than a hundred yards, giving it considerable weight, and would have to be securely anchored so as to be able to support the additional weight of snow and ice or the force of strong wind.

The distance from the Hardman house to the nearest telephone pole was, Larry estimated, between eighty and a hundred yards. To the Chevy coupe, his destination, it was half that distance. The two most difficult spots would be just as he left the roof and the wire took his weight for the first time, and the two or three yards he had to pass over the gorge, where a slip could be fatal.

Other than that, if he was careful, the trip should be easy. The wire would support him. The connection to the house seemed strong enough. It would hold him, if necessary. But of course, he realized, this was all hypothetical. It assumed he would have to make the trip. And he would not because Kenny would be arriving at any moment. Kenny would come bursting through the woods, shouting obscenities, shooting into the air, loving every minute of it.

But he would always know he could have saved them, Larry thought to himself, if he had been forced to. That was important.

The return trip across the roof was easier than he had expected. The shingles had been loosened, the snow pushed away, so he had both a solid foothold and grip. It was all easy, and so he became overconfident, moving more quickly as he got closer to the window.

It happened suddenly, and it was not totally his fault. Six feet from the window he'd grabbed the edge of a shingle with his left hand, tested it, and only then released his right hand grip and begun pulling across.

The shingle tore loose. Without warning he found himself gliding down the few feet of roof on a slide of soft snow, the torn remnants of the shingle still tightly gripped in his left hand. Desperately he slammed his bare feet into the snow, his right hand searching for something solid. Somehow he found another loose shingle and desperately grasped, almost stopping, but his grip was not strong enough. He moved in a steady slow-motion slide that he was powerless to stop.

Finally, his feet slipped off the edge of the roof and for a split second floated freely in midair. But then his toes stuck in the gutter that surrounded the house. His weight pulled it loose from the side of the house with an eerie squeal. But it held.

At first he dared not breathe. He lay absolutely still against the roof. Despite the cold, beads of sweat popped through his skin. His fervent wish was to lie there in precarious safety forever.

He tried lifting his head; the gutter squeaked and moved a bit farther away from the house. If the gutter ripped free he would drop into the yard. Again he lifted his head, this time removing his left foot from the gutter and pushing it against the roof as hard as he could. Nothing happened.

Slowly, carefully, he looked up. The open window was only inches from his outstretched hand. With one great push upward he could probably reach it.

With a screech, the gutter pulled away another inch.

Larry unsuccessfully tried to pry a shingle loose with the tips of his fingers, and suddenly realized all choice was gone. He would have to gamble and push off the gutter hard enough to propel his body upward those few inches. He knew it would work.

He knew it would never work. What was the alternative? Call Diane? Have her try to pull him in? Even that might not work. And the thought of her knowing he had failed again was abominable.

Where the hell was Kenny, anyway? Goddamn him.

Why wasn't he there to help! What in hell was keeping him?

He exhaled. Ten. Nine. He started counting down, gathering his remaining energy. Six. Five. He would bend his legs, push off hard, claw his way to the window. Two. One.

Thrusting with all his might, he folded himself into a ball then exploded upward. The gutter ripped from the house with a final screech, but it had held just long enough to give him support. He grabbed for the window frame, barely catching it, then brought his left leg up. And fell hard into the attic.

Diane clambered up the ladder frantically, but he was already safe when she reached him. Safe. They would not get at him. Not this time.

Frieda listened intently to the sounds above her, only relaxing when she heard the mumbled voices. Her kitchen seemed bigger than ever before, the whole house seemed bigger—and colder. It was Thomas' absence, of course, she knew that. She picked up a salt-shaker and examined it, noticing the little Dutch girl seemed to have her eyes closed. Or maybe they had just worn away. It was difficult to know, everything was suddenly so different.

The worn collar that the golden retriever had been wearing caught her eye. It was lying in the corner, where Larry had thrown it. Frieda picked it up, fingering it almost tenderly. The metal plate on the collar was rust-encrusted, but by rubbing with her nail she managed to loosen some of the caked rust. "My name is DOLLY," she read, "and I belong to the LANGSAM family. If I'm lost, please call 555-3909."

If I'm lost, she read again, her eyes filling with tears.

ELEVEN

"I called the police again," Diane explained. "They said tomorrow."

Larry peeled off his wet shirt and dropped it onto the floor.

"When do you think Kenny'll get here?"

He stripped off his wet pants and underpants, dropping them in a pile next to the shirt. "I'm not sure he'll get here at all, Diane," he said finally, without looking at her. "I think Kenny is irresponsible, and we can't depend on him, that's what I think."

"And so what do. . . ."

"What we do," he interrupted her brusquely, "is wait. We wait for the police, or the Coast Guard, or Superman or whoever the hell gets over here first!" Although he was dry, and warm in the dry clothes, he still could not stop shaking.

Diane did not seem to notice. "Larry," she began in her now-I'm-going-to-tell-you-something-New York-best-bitch tone, "that dog bit your son. And I don't . . . I don't. . . ." Her voice broke completely. "Larry, do something," she pleaded in a high, shrill voice. "I just don't know what to do. Don't you understand? I don't know what to do? His wrist is turning all colors and, Larry, I'm so afraid."

He moved to her and folded her into his arms. She needed him. Finally. *She* needed *him*. Her words were almost incoherent as she tried to verbalize her jumbled thoughts. The possibility of rabies terrified her. Long needles jabbing into Josh. Weeks of pain. And then only if they got him to the hospital in time. How much time was enough time? A day? A week? Could it possibly be too late already? "They're never coming," she mumbled, "we'll never get out of here. Never ever. Do something, Larry, do something, please, please, please!"

The dogs had won. He was no longer ashamed to admit that. The pack of dogs was too much for him to defeat alone. But the dogs had had great luck. The storm bypassing the island. The neighbors leaving. Even the goddamn Greek freighter going aground at just the wrong time. Luck and fate. Temporarily, they had won, but he was not yet ready to surrender.

This lull was not a surrender. He was merely exercising extreme caution. It was the only way to live; caution ensured life itself. He would live to fight them again, and wasn't that what life was all about: survival! Even his buildings, tall and strong; his houses, plain but sturdy, reflected this. That had been at the heart of his success. Durability.

Diane was having trouble catching her breath. ". . . frightened, so frightened, help. . . ."

That had been a close call on the roof, and he was lucky the gutter held as long as it did. Luck! Luck, again? That's the one element you can't rely on. You must have a plan, complete to every movement. And in the end the dogs would have to lose because their success depended on continued luck. It was just a matter of time. All they had to do was wait. Just wait.

God, how could he go out there again? It was just not possible. It was too much to ask of him. Diane snuggled close to him, holding him fiercely. He couldn't go out there again.

But as he held her, breathing the perfume of her hair, he knew he could do nothing else. The pack had finally pulled him from the house.

Taking her forearms and pushing her from him, he kissed her hard on the mouth. "It's okay," he whispered, "I'm going for the car now. Do you understand?"

Diane looked at him quizzically for a moment, then nodded affirmatively.

"Get everybody dressed warmly and downstairs. Keep the kitchen door locked until I pull the car up right next to the house. I'll pull close enough so the dogs won't be able to get between the car and the house. Do you hear me?"

Again she nodded blankly.

"Good. Remember to bring the paper bag from the refrigerator. We need that to show the doctors. Do you understand?"

"Yes," she said weakly.

He dressed as warmly as he could, pulling a thick wool sweater over the Calvin Klein cashmere Diane had given him last Christmas. He took a second belt from his suitcase and fastened it loosely around his waist. He would succeed, there was no question of that, but it would be dangerous and there was really no reason for him to go at all. Help would arrive. Tomorrow, the day after, whenever. But eventually it would arrive. Then why?

For Diane, he told himself. And, after pausing, admitted silently, for myself.

Diane followed him downstairs. There was very little of the chic New York City model still recognizable. Her eyes were red and puffy, large brown circles half closed them. Her hair was disheveled, her clothes badly wrinkled. And Larry loved her more at that moment than he had for years.

In the hall closet he found his mother's red cloth coat, and in the right pocket, the keys to the Chevy. He took the fireplace poker from the living room and in the kitchen, after giving his mother a reassuring touch, collected a sharp carving knife and two long pieces of rope, all of which were added to his hammer. With that peculiar store of equipment dangling from his body he stood at the top of the stairs and announced, "I'm ready."

Diane inspected him as he stood before her in his bare feet. The knife was stuck through his belt on his right side, the hammer on his left. The second belt was loosely fastened around his waist. The two lengths of rope hung over his left shoulder, and he held the fireplace poker in his right hand.

"Not exactly standard mountain-climbing gear," he commented.

Diane smiled for the first time in days. "Larry," she began, but he did not let her finish.

"I'll be okay," he said reassuringly. "Just get ready downstairs, and don't forget the bag."

She hugged him. "No, I won't."

With the knife handle digging into his thigh, he climbed to the attic for the final time. He was leaving this house. Getting his family out. By himself!

He crawled onto the windowsill and looked out at the pack lazing in the yard. The sky was still overcast and threatening, but it hadn't snowed and the temperature had risen somewhat. Briefly, just before taking the first step onto the snow, he closed his eyes and saw them again, racing across the snow, charging, then dragging the old man down. Once again, he heard the dreadful sound of human flesh being ripped from the bone.

Hatred surged through his body. He was ready. His passage was easier this time, the snow having been cleared and the shingles loosened on the previous trip, although the additional equipment made it painful to lie flush against the roof. He worked his way carefully toward the wire. It was almost over.

Water from the snow melted by the warmth of his body soaked through his clothing, but he did not feel it. His mind focused on the wire and the dogs and nothing else.

He reached the connection and lay on the edge of the

roof. There was no time to consider his accomplishment. There was only hard work to be done and he set to it, working quickly, each movement carried out with great care.

He stretched out his right leg for balance, drove the knife into the roof for support, and pulled the wire to him. Removing the second belt from around his waist, he looped it around the wire. Then he attached the buckle of that belt, a brown Ted Lapidus, a gift from Diane on his last birthday, to the leather end of the black belt in his pants, locking them together by pushing the thin metal tongue of the brown belt through the first punched hole of the black belt. Then he repeated the process, locking the holed end of the brown belt to the buckle of the black belt. When he was finished he had a makeshift safety line, with the wire trapped inside.

Next, he took one length of rope and tied it to his ankles, carefully leaving eighteen inches of slack between them. He then spread his legs apart until the eighteen-inch length was taut, and rested it on top of the telephone wire. Cautiously, he lowered his legs until he ran out of rope. They hung suspended, one on either side, nine inches below the wire. The rope lay across the wire and supported his weight.

Still working from the corner of the roof, he looped the second piece of rope around his upper back, bringing it just under his armpits, then over the top of the wire before knotting it tightly, and creating a third makeshift sling to hold him to the wire. With that rope around his chest, the two belts holding him at the waist, and the second length of rope supporting his feet, he had constructed a cradle that would allow him to slide down the wire while keeping his hands free and his weight evenly distributed.

He looked once more at his goal, the car. The pack was moving about the yard, but did not seem greatly interested in the action on the roof. Taking the fireplace poker in his right hand, and holding tightly to the knife punched into the roof with his left hand, he stretched his legs out along the telephone wire for the first time. As he suspected it would, the rope slid along the wire easily. There seemed to be almost no friction. The wire jumped up and down and a few small ice particles fell off and dropped into the snow.

After the wire had ceased bouncing, Larry released his grip on the knife and caterpillared his body forward until his legs hung free on the wire, and his rump balanced just on the edge of the roof. Leaning far forward, and gripping the wire firmly in both his hands, he pulled himself off the roof. His body fell free for an instant, until all slack from the ropes and belt was gone, then bounced to a halt. The wire sagged, and danced crazily and he squeezed it between his hands. But it held him. For a moment he dared not move, waiting until all was still, just hanging precariously in midair, far above the pack.

Bob Pledge, chewing diligently on a ragged toothpick, took one look at the boat and announced he would not make the trip. "Not in that, Ken," he said, gesturing with his hands in disgust, "it just won't cut it in rough water."

Twenty-one-year-old Rick Berkow, owner, captain and complete crew of the aging craft, spoke up in its defense. "I'm telling you, it'll make it." No up-country coward was going to cheat him out of the $250 he'd quoted for a one-day rental. No way.

Taking the pick from his mouth and carefully examining it, Pledge asked, "And how old are you, son?"

"Twenty-one," Berkow answered defensively, "almost twenty-two."

Pledge looked at Kenny. "And he's been running these waters his whole life." Pledge threw the pick to the ground and said derisively, "Sheeeet!"

The *Rita Baby* was a small, wooden-hull cruiser powered by two Evinrude inboards. Although a large crack across the plastic windshield and badly peeling baby-blue paint appeared to be her only obvious defects, the *Rita Baby* reeked of years of overuse and undercare.

"Com'on, Bob," Kenny pleaded, "you don't think I'm gonna take any chance with my life, do you? I know boats, I been around boats all my life, this baby's in great shape. You think I'd pay two hundred bucks for a boat that wasn't safe?"

"Two-fifty," Berkow corrected him.

Kenny nodded agreement. "Two-fifty." It was only money after all, and Larry would pay him back. That was only fair, he recognized, because in his own way, he was using this trip to pay Larry back. For everything.

Berkow had been working the counter in the coffee shop and, after the fishermen departed, came to the table and introduced himself, explaining he knew of a boat that might serve their needs. "The only reason it's still in the water this late," he told them, "is that this guy is building a house over on Shelter Island, and we've been using it to run supplies out there. It'll take all of you, no problem."

"You skipper?" Kenny had asked.

With a shrug of his shoulder toward the bald-headed short-order cook behind the counter, Berkow said, "Can't. Gotta stay here with him. But I'll rent it to you for a couple of days."

They had made the deal on the spot, and Pledge had raised no objections until he saw *Rita Baby* bouncing in the rough water. "I'm just not going," he repeated. "I'm sorry, but I don't believe this thing is fit."

"For Christ sakes, Bobby, don't be such a pussy," Hirschfeld said scornfully. "It just needs a paint job. Then it would look fine and you wouldn't be opening your yap."

"Don't talk to me that way, Len," Pledge said measuredly. "And don't tell me what I see with my own damn eyes. This boat isn't safe and I'll be damned if I'm gonna risk my life in it."

Len took a step toward him, the beer rumbling in his gut giving him courage. Kenny cut between them. "Okay, Bob, you stay here. We're only going to be gone a few hours anyway. We'll be back this afternoon. Len and I can handle it easy, all we got to do is shoot us a few dogs. Right, Len?"

Len agreed as to how that was "absolutely correct. We don't need him anyway!"

They took the rifles, handguns and ammunition from the rear of the Rover, carried them aboard the *Rita Baby*, packed them under a flotation cushion where they would hopefully stay dry, donned the oily-smelling yellow slickers Berkow supplied, and slowly pushed out into the bay waters.

The first four-foot wave hit them less than seventy feet from the dock and sent the *Rita Baby's* bow high into the air. The boat banged hard back into the water, soaking them with a heavy spray. "We're gonna get wet," Kenny shouted gleefully, over the roar of the twin engines.

"So I noticed," Hirschfeld shouted back, the beer in his belly rolling around like unleashed cargo.

Diane tried to do exactly as her husband had ordered. She dressed the children warmly and brought them downstairs to wait in the living room. Marcy was cranky and hungry, and close to tears. Josh then made things worse by hitting her for being a crybaby.

Frieda put on her red cloth coat and waited silently in the living room with Diane. Corny was quite willing to move downstairs after Diane carried all her magazine cutouts down for her.

Diane was beginning to feel better after her outburst. It had released much of the emotion that had been pent up inside her, but as she and her mother-in-law stared out the window, watching the bouncing telephone cable, she wondered if it had really been worth it. "I made him go out there," she said matter-of-factly.

"No, I'm sure you didn't," Frieda answered benevolently.

"I did. I shamed him into it. I didn't leave him any choice." The dawning recognition of that truth was painful.

Larry's feet moved into view, hanging from the wire as in some strange circus. Diane was surprised how clearly his unshod feet and dark pants stood out against the dreary sky.

Momentarily a vision of her son floated across Frieda's mind. Larry, standing at the base of a big tree, screaming dire imprecations up at Kenny, perched precariously on a branch. Larry never managed to get up that tree, Kenny never really came down. Two brothers, so different.

Larry seemed awkward and out of place dangling from that telephone wire, and Frieda suddenly knew that he would not make it. Knowing that, she could no longer watch, and turned back into the kitchen.

Diane could just see the top of the car above the slats of the wooden fence that guarded the gorge. Just as Larry had explained, the telephone wire stretched directly over it. Gradually, pulling, pushing, Larry moved steadily closer. He looked incredibly foolish hanging in midair, the wire sagging under his weight. Small puffs of white mist came from his mouth at regular intervals. Her attention was so riveted on him that she failed to notice the dogs beginning to move toward the wire.

The cold had reached the shepherd. The hours of waiting in the snow, maintaining control over the pack and the loneliness had benumbed him. But now, as he again saw movement on the roof, he understood that the waiting had ended.

The Labrador sat up as the first snow particles fluttered from the roof, then took three hesitant steps toward the house. The shepherd noticed the Labrador's advance and growled threateningly. Then the shepherd acted. He trotted toward the black dog, baring his teeth in a snarl, leaving no doubt he would go for the Labrador if it continued its challenge to his leadership. The Labrador took a tentative step toward the shepherd, then turned away, resuming his place.

The shepherd concentrated once more on the roof. He would meet this challenge alone.

He moved across the yard to a position near the wire. He did not know what the enemy intended to do, but he knew instinctively the ultimate confrontation was close at hand.

He's waiting, Larry thought, as he maneuvered down the wire. The knowledge of the approaching struggle actually made him feel good.

The other dogs stirred and set up a yelping which seemed to have no real purpose save to make noise. The hours in the yard had been long, cold and boring. But the shepherd had provided for them, and they trusted him.

Larry was out over the yard now. There was nothing beneath him to break his fall if he slipped, he realized, and his only path back to the safety of the house on the ground was through the dogs. The prospect no longer frightened him as once it had.

He moved down the wire another few feet, slowly inching his way, stretching his legs out as far as possible, reaching forward with his hands, pulling his body forward to meet his legs, then pushing out again down the wire with his legs. The ropes and interlocked belts held, sliding easily along the wire.

At the window Diane locked her hands together until her knuckles whitened. She realized suddenly that she was breathing in unison with the small white puffs coming from her husband's mouth. The wire bounced crazily, strangely reminding her of a runaway guitar string. And then she saw the gray shepherd. The dog stood directly under Larry, nervously wagging its tail, staring up at the wire. Its mouth was open, tongue lolling, saliva dripping onto the stained snow. She could not distinguish its voice from those of the rest of the barking pack, but if she had, she would have noticed its howl had become a pleading whine.

The enemy was coming closer to the ground with every movement along the black wire. The man scent was overwhelming, and the shepherd could hear the sound of his harsh, rapid breathing. But the man was too high to be reached. The dog could not leap to that height. And so he would have to be patient a little longer.

Larry was moving steadily along the wire, the primitive procedure, the makeshift method, working very well. Slowly, carefully, painfully. His neck was throbbing with pain, and occasionally he would allow his head to droop. But too much blood rushed into his brain, temporarily making him dizzy, so he relaxed for only brief periods. Larry-look-before-you-leap Kenny had once called him. No more. Not after this. Now it was Kenny who had proven to be the failure.

Gradually, as he reached the midpoint of the yard, the pack grew quiet, and the only sound in the yard was the gray shepherd's low, pleading whine. Larry shifted the poker from his right hand to his left, taking time to twist his head to look down. For the first time he saw the shepherd waiting impatiently directly below him.

Their eyes met. Larry stared into the shepherd's alert black eyes and felt his stomach muscles tighten. The shepherd opened its mouth and whined. Come down, Larry heard him saying, come down.

Larry laughed to himself, knowing this to be a deadly game. The dog could not lure him from the wire. Soon he would reach the car. And then he would kill the dog. He despised the dog, but killing it was a matter of survival.

Larry hung suspended in his makeshift cradle watching the dog. It was difficult to believe that so beautiful an animal could be so deadly. That man's first, and best animal friend, could also be his murderer. As the wire stopped shaking, Larry reached out and seized it, and moved a few inches closer to safety.

On the ground, directly below him, the dog followed his progress.

Larry brushed his head against his shoulder, wiping away some of the sweat that had collected on his forehead. His hands were sore from gripping the rubber wire. His neck ached. His bandaged thigh was throbbing. His scratched eye itched constantly. And he was exhausted.

The shepherd barked, sending a shiver through Larry's body.

Not yet, you bastard, he thought, I'm not finished yet. He moved another six inches closer to the car. Looking down, he screamed, "Don't smile, you bastard! Don't you dare!"

His fatigue was overwhelming, and he began to cheat, not quite finishing each pull. It cost him a few inches from each thrust, but he was still moving forward.

Larry was only nine feet from the wooden fence when the shepherd leaped into the air for the first time. It was not as if the dog expected to reach the enemy but rather was releasing pent-up energy. The dog jumped a second time, just barely pushing off his hind legs and rising only a few inches off the snow-covered ground.

Behind him, the pack began to react to its leader's actions. The Labrador moved closer to the wolfhound.

The boxer pushed next to the shivering dalmatian and the bored setter. But only the feisty dachshund dared approach the shepherd, to be completely ignored, and eventually forced to retreat. The dogs sensed the end of their wait.

Diane's breath clouded the window and she had to wipe the moisture away continually in order to see out. Larry was still making slow progress, but now the shepherd seemed greatly agitated. Its leaps, although somehow tentative, were strong but thus far fell short of the wire.

Frieda closed her eyes and listened. The howling animals would tell her when something happened, she did not have to see it. Desperately she tried to concentrate on happy memories but to no avail. The thought of Larry risking his life on the wire was impossible to overcome. Is life worth this suffering? she wondered. She did not try to answer her own question.

Larry refused to look down again but doing so really wasn't necessary. The dog was there. There was no doubt about that. For the rest of his life, the dog would always be there.

The shepherd realized his enemy was slowing since his own progress toward the wooden fence had slowed. He was often forced to sit and wait while the enemy rested motionless above him. So close. So unreachable. The shepherd's whines became more urgent as it sensed that confrontation was near. Saliva dribbled from his tongue, lathering like foam against his fur. He could taste this enemy.

The car was close now. Larry could see bits of black paint on the side panels where the snow had melted. When he reached the coupe he would have to move quickly to untie the two ropes and the belt and get inside before the dogs realized they could get at him over the bridge. As soon as he touched down on the roof of the car, or maybe the hood would be better, he would have to leap off, into the snow. Onto the ground with them. There was no alternative.

Once inside the car he would have a weapon to use against them. A weapon? Literally, a tank. Let them try to keep him isolated here. That would be fine. He would use his weapon to drive them into the ground. Especially the shepherd. That gray monster had to die. It could not be allowed to live after the crimes it had committed. If it did not die today, Larry knew he would have to return to the island and hunt it down. He could never, ever, live at peace knowing the shepherd was alive.

Thrusting out with his legs again, he gained a few more precious inches.

The dog watched as his enemy approached the protection of the wooden fence and understood it would have to attack soon. The longer he waited, though, the lower the enemy would be on the wire. So he watched Larry inch slowly along the cable, poised for his spring.

But there was nothing the dog could do. Larry was going to make it to the car. And once in the car, he could bring his family to the safety of the brick buildings in the small town. At the first break in the storm he would launch the powerboat the islanders kept in a watershed year round for emergencies, and island-hop to safety. From Burrows to Gardiners to Orient Point. He could easily handle the boat by himself, that part of his island upbringing could never be forgotten.

Two yards from the top of the fence Larry realized he was going to make it.

The dog made his first real jump when Larry was only five feet from the fence. Suddenly pushing off with all the power in his hind legs, he shot four or five feet into the air, paws flailing at Larry's back.

Larry did not even realize the dog had jumped until he heard it fall back into the snow.

As soon as the shepherd's legs hit the ground, he struggled to regain his balance and launched himself into the air again. This time he came closer, but still almost a foot short. The shepherd fell back, only to rise and leap again. And again.

Larry twisted his head and looked down at the shepherd.

The dog hurtled closer, snapping its jaws. Larry took a moment to calm the pounding of his heart, then returned to his work.

The dog leaped again, howling savagely. It seemed to know it would not be able to reach him, and so it jumped again, desperately, but its legs were rapidly losing their strength, and its leaps fell shorter, even as the enemy sagged lower.

The setter and the boxer came loping across the yard to aid the leader. But halfway across, the Labrador trotted in front of the other dogs and halted them, understanding that the shepherd had to have this enemy alone, or lose the pack.

The image of Thomas Hardman buried under the pack flashed through Larry's mind.

The dog twisted his great body as he projected himself high into the air. Now it was the shepherd who had lost control, making one mad leap after another, clawing desperately at the empty air.

Larry's legs were just over the fence. With a couple of more pulls he would be over the gorge. Free. Safe.

He could ignore the shepherd no longer.

Smiling, he took the poker in his right hand and tightened his grip. As the shepherd leaped once again into the air Larry turned his body and swung it at the dog's head.

The poker whizzed by the dog's skull, missing by inches.

The dog lay on the ground, its tail between its rear legs, ears down. Defeated. Larry pulled himself forward another few inches as the dog gathered himself for one final leap. Larry gripped the poker firmly, trying to time the dog's jump.

The dog pushed off and catapulted toward him.

Larry started swinging as the dog left the ground, and the poker sliced through empty air. At the top of its leap, the shepherd snapped, and this time his jaws caught Larry's right wrist. The poker fell harmlessly to the ground as the shepherd buried its teeth into the wrist. And hung on.

TWELVE

Nervously Kenny watched the rising swells sweep toward them from deep water but was totally unprepared when the *Rita Baby* capsized. The boat plowed into a submerged object, lurched into the air and plunged prow-first into the trough of a wave. There had been no warning. One second Kenny had been standing at the wheel, legs spread wide apart for balance on the slippery deck. Then he was flipped into the air, out and over the left side, finally crashing head first into the freezing waters of Long Island Sound.

He went under, taking a mouthful of salty water, and desperately fought his way to the surface. He began frantically searching for the boat. But a larger wave smashed into his face, choking off his breath and dragging him down. His hunting boots filled with water, anchoring him. Without panicking, he ripped them off and clawed upward again, holding his breath until he burst above the surface to feel the freezing air wash over his face.

The boat! Keep calm and find the boat. At first he

couldn't see it, and he became terrified by the thought that it had sunk. Without the boat, without something to cling to, he was dead. But when a wave lifted him, he spotted the boat thirty yards away, the overturned hull drifting sluggishly through the heavy water away from him. A gush of hissing steam poured from its stern, the last gasp of dying engines. Kenny began swimming for his life. The boat floated lazily away from him, the thirty yards becoming forty. He pushed his body through the water, hands knifing through the surface, legs pumping furiously. The waves held him back, then shoved him forward and gradually the gap closed. He did not think, he worked. Stroke after stroke through the angry water.

He finally managed to grab hold of one of the narrow curved planks that formed the hull. The overlapping slats provided thin steps and Kenny scrambled up onto the hull. He had swallowed a lot of murky water, but had survived.

His weight forced the boat lower in the water, and frequently it swooped down into a hollow between waves and salt water washed over him. But he had solid footing, and by leaning forward he managed to keep a low center of gravity. He had no idea how long the hull would float. A few hours at best, he guessed. Unless the storm worsened. Then it would not last minutes.

Something brushed the stern of the boat with a soft thud. He turned, but there was nothing. The boat soared atop another wave, then slid down easily. As it did, Kenny saw a bright yellow rain slicker floating open on the surface like a leaf, hiding a substantial weight underneath. He began crawling back on the hull, but as he got close to the stern the boat dipped precariously, and he decided against moving further. There was nothing he could do but watch with fascination as the slicker and its hidden weight floated alongside the boat. Then, abruptly, it disappeared.

Len?

Beer-bellied Len? Ole laugh-a-minute Len? Floating like a goddamn cork? Dead? Impossible. How much time had passed since the boat went over? Five minutes? Ten at most. He couldn't be sure. He desperately searched the horizon, twisting, trying to watch all sides as the boat lifted, then dropped. He had forgotten about Len. Saved himself and forgotten Len. Maybe Len could have been saved. Maybe that wasn't even Len.

"Len!" It was stupid to shout, the water smothered his loudest shouts. "Lenny!" What the hell else was there to do?

The boat slid off another wave crest, but as it fell Kenny thought for an instant that he saw a second spot of yellow buried behind another wave. When the hull rose again he scanned the area. Nothing.

Then it was there again. The second bright yellow raincoat drifting in the water. This time he could see hands protruding from the yellow arms, and a dark head flat in the water. Lenny! But the boat was drifting in the wrong direction, away from the body.

He thought he saw a hand reach out.

But it was so far away. Straddling the hull, Kenny stood up. Now he could see a little better. The body was face up.

The hand moved again. There could be no mistaking it. Goddamn Lenny was still alive.

Kenny looked around the hull for something, anything, to propel it toward the floating figure. But there was nothing. Len floated farther away. He couldn't just let him go, not that way, watch your buddy's ass, that's what they taught him in Nam, watch your goddamn buddy's ass. Stripping off his pants and shirt, Kenny took a mouthful of air, then dived into the swirling waters.

Diane watched the grotesque tableau unfold in silent horror. The shepherd held Larry's right wrist in its teeth and hung, dangling slowly in the air. The wire sagged slowly stretching, dropping the dog's hind legs closer to the ground. Larry held onto the wire as best he could with his left hand and frantically tried to yank his right hand free. But the dog held his wrist in a viselike grip.

The rope and belts did not give. They held Larry to the wire as firmly as the weight of the dog pulled him from it. With a small pop a sharp stinging pain exploded in his right shoulder as muscles tore.

Larry screamed.

Diane closed her eyes as her husband's scream ripped through her.

He let go of the wire with his left hand and tried to reach across his body to strike at the dog. His blow just barely grazed the dog's black muzzle.

The shepherd's eyes bulged and it uttered a peculiar gurgling sound. Gradually, steadily, the rubber-encased wire stretched under the additional weight and the dog and the man sank nearer the ground. The shepherd's legs were only nine inches away from the ground when the wire finally snapped.

Diane covered her mouth to hold her scream as the broken cable cracked like a whip.

The shepherd hit the ground first, attempting to scramble to its feet as Larry's legs crashed heavily onto the top slat of the wooden fence and he tumbled backward into the snow. As he did his legs slammed into the dog, stunning it. The shepherd recovered almost immediately and pounced. Larry crossed his right arm in front of his body, punching with his free hand, but the injured muscles made his right arm useless.

The gray shepherd tore at him savagely, catching his right biceps in its teeth and tearing a piece of flesh from the bone. Blood spurted from the open wound, splashing the dog, but it pressed the attack.

Larry managed to regain his footing, but the rope tied around his ankles sent him sprawling again. The dog would give him no chance, pursuing its maniacal attack, growling, jumping, biting, tearing.

Diane grabbed the first knife she found and yanked open the kitchen door. But she managed only two steps into the yard.

The Labrador and Irish setter stood ten feet from her and, though they made no attempt to move toward the house, their presence forced her to retreat. Their message was clear; they would not interfere with the battle, they would permit no one else to. The sound of the one-sided fight flooded the air as she backed slowly into the kitchen.

Sensing the kill, the shepherd had pounced on Larry's chest, snapping viciously at his face. In its frenzy, the dog planted its front leg on Larry's windpipe, digging its claws into his neck and cutting off his breathing. Desperately, Larry grabbed at the offending paw with his good hand.

He held the tip of the shepherd's forepaw in his left hand and squeezed as hard as his strength allowed. As he did, the dog began to whine. Its teeth tightly clenched together, the dog shoved its muzzle against Larry's hand, trying to gnaw himself free. The harder Larry squeezed, mashing the tender bones in the foreleg, the more the dog suffered.

Larry had accidentally discovered a point of great vulnerability. Because of the intense pain in the forepaw, the shepherd could no longer bite.

Gingerly, without easing the pressure, Larry lifted the leg from his throat and rose to his knees, and then, pulling the dog upright with him, onto his feet. Slowly, the strange pair began backing toward the house.

Diane stood at the kitchen door, holding it open. The other dogs remained still. Only the dachshund rushed at Larry, snapping at his ankles.

They were fifteen yards from the door when the shepherd finally tore free of Larry's grip and made one final attack, relentlessly hurling its blood-covered body at him. Larry was almost at the door when the shepherd found an opening. The dog gripped Larry's forearm and the yard echoed to the snap of bone. Instinctively Larry kicked out, and caught the dog low in the groin. The shepherd collapsed into the snow, writhing in pain.

Diane half pulled, half dragged her husband inside the kitchen. "Okay," he managed to say, then lost consciousness.

She slammed and bolted the door before turning to her husband. The shreds of his wool sweater dripped blood. His right arm was torn open and she could see the white of exposed bone. An involuntary shiver ran the length of his body and she realized he was in shock.

Frieda stood helplessly watching her son, while Diane acted quickly to save his life. She pulled the red-and-white-checked cloth from the kitchen table, sending a flowered sugar jar smashing onto the floor, and wrapped it tightly around his arm to stem the flow of blood. "Get me a shirt!" she screamed at Frieda. "Hurry."

The tiny white squares of the table cloth were turning pink, then red, and the red squares were deepening. Diane pulled the cloth tighter, but it was too bulky to be really useful. "It'll be all right," she whispered, "Larry, it'll be all right."

He opened his eyes and she could read the pain there. "It hurts," he said weakly. "It hurts."

Frieda came back with two brightly colored sports shirts. Diane slit the sleeve from one of them. Gently lifting Larry's right arm, she slipped the sleeve under his biceps, pulled it around, then tied it as tightly as she could. Then she cut off the other sleeve and tied that just above his elbow. Working quickly, she cut the shirt into two pieces. The first she wrapped just below his elbow, and with the other bound the gaping wound in his wrist.

"Will Daddy be all right?" Josh asked. She had forgotten the children, unaware that they had entered the kitchen.

"Yes," she said, "but go upstairs."

"But, Mama," Josh started to protest.

"Go!" It was an order and the child left the kitchen.

The four tourniquets seemed to stop the flow of blood, but his arm was so bloody that it was all but impossible to see how bad his wounds really were. Wetting a clean cloth, she wiped away as much blood as she could and inspected the arm closely. Small, round teeth punctures covered almost its entire length. Bone showed in two different spots. A long slice of skin had been torn free and now lay loosely on the arm, barely covering the two sections of the snapped ulna. The arm, she realized, was very bad, but most of the bleeding had been stopped.

Once she had cleansed and bandaged his right arm, Diane methodically searched the rest of Larry's body for additional wounds. There were many. She ripped the second shirt apart and began bandaging those which still bled. A nasty tear on his left wrist flowed steadily. The cloth that had covered his right thigh was gone and another piece of flesh had been torn from the first wound. A shallow cut on one side of his buttock bled copiously. Teeth marks dotted both his legs. She cut the lengths of rope from his ankles and chest, and cleaned and bound his wounds.

In the time it required for Diane to work over the rest of his body, Larry's right arm had turned a pinkish-white. The undamaged tissues, she realized, were not getting enough blood. Cautiously, she loosened the tourniquets, one after another, watching closely to see if blood poured from his wounds. The bleeding had ceased completely in some places, although blood still seeped thinly in others.

But with the tourniquets loosened a bit, the arm began to regain a little natural color.

Larry seemed to be unconscious. His eyes were clamped shut, but his breathing remained steady. Diane knew she had to keep working. If she stopped even momentarily, if she allowed herself time to worry, she might lose control. The work kept her mind free of the worst fears, so as long as he kept breathing she would continue working.

There was so much that had to be done. It was vital to keep him out of shock and she thought she knew the simple rules for that. Raise the head and lower the legs. Or was it raise the legs and lower the head? No longer sure, she made up her own rules. She placed two thick pillows from the living room couch under his right arm, reasoning that the higher it was, the less blood he would lose. Then she placed two additional pillows under his legs and propped a final one under his head, hopefully making it as easy as possible for blood to flow to his heart. Then she covered him with two blankets. Keeping him warm was important, of that much she was certain.

But the harder Diane worked, the more obvious the truth became; if Larry did not get professional medical help soon he would die. He had lost a lot of blood and even if he did get help quickly, she feared he might lose his right arm. It looked so badly mangled it didn't seem possible any amount of repair could make it work again. Yet the realization did not shock her, or send her into hysterics. She was past that, there was simply no time for it. He would have help or he would die. And until one or the other happened, she would sit at his side on the hard kitchen floor and keep him as warm and comfortable as possible.

Frieda had done the fetching for Diane. Gotten blankets. Brought pillows. Collected bandages. Searched for antiseptic. Occasionally she glanced outside to check on the pack. The dogs seemed to be stirring, but their movements appeared aimless and they came no nearer to the house.

Her son and daughter-in-law had come to the island for a vacation. They had brought her grandchildren. It should have been a joyous time, a time for love. Tom had so looked forward to their coming, even knowing that he would argue with his son about.... Her mind blanked out. Tom? Out there? And they had done this to Larry. Her rage was fueled by the helplessness she felt. They had no right!

The gray shepherd was exhausted rather than hurt. The enemy's kick had stunned him and left him with a throbbing pain in his gut, but otherwise he was not injured. He sat near the house, apart from the pack, waiting to see if the enemy would return.

He was hungry. It had not occurred to him to eat while he had been standing guard, but the action of the last few minutes had left him ravenous. He dug his muzzle into the trampled snow and recovered a piece of the heretofore forbidden, now frozen meat. Holding it between his front paws, he tore away at it, gulping down the shreds he managed to tear off.

The Irish setter joined him and began sniffing. If the leader was hurt, if he could no longer lead, that must be known quickly. The pack could not survive without a strong, capable leader.

The shepherd allowed the setter to approach him, lick the blood glued to his back and inspect the food he was eating. Only when the shepherd had finished the chunk of meat did he emit a low, threatening growl.

The setter did not react. The sound itself contained no meaning. The pack must be shown the shepherd was still capable of fighting.

The shepherd was ready. He sprang forward, set his

front paws wide apart in the burrowed snow, and bared his teeth in a savage snarl. Before the setter could move back the shepherd snapped at it, barely missing its front leg. He would fight for the right to lead his pack.

The setter returned to its place and began burrowing into the snow for meat. The other dogs followed suit. The pack would wait, but inevitably the shepherd's leadership would be tested again.

Kenny swam boldly through the white-capped water, aiming for the spot where he'd last seen the floating body, changing direction each time he managed a quick glimpse of the yellow slicker. The current carried Len to Kenny's right, and it took more minutes of hard swimming to catch up with him. Every few strokes Kenny would stop, tread water, and recheck the distance back to the hull.

Len Hirschfeld was barely alive when Kenny reached him. A pocket of air had been trapped under the yellow slicker, and it was this that had kept him afloat. But his eyes closed and he drifted aimlessly on the angry water, seemingly having surrendered to the whims of the Sound. Kenny threw an arm lock around Hirschfeld's neck, hoping to prevent him from fighting back in panic. Len made a weak effort to resist, then gave up, probably even before he understood this hold on the slicker collar. "Can you swim?" Kenny shouted.

"My leg," Hirschfeld screamed back, "my leg."

He would not swim, but Kenny could not tell whether he was able to do so or not. Clutching the slicker, Kenny began to struggle toward the overturned hull. Len had been in the cold water much too long already.

They barely made it and, when they did, Kenny had no strength left to hoist the overweight Hirschfeld up onto the capsized craft. "Climb up!" he yelled.

"Help me," Hirschfeld blubbered, "help me, Kenny."

Laboriously Kenny turned him around and pushed him face first against the hull, so that his body and his outstretched arms rested against the boat's side. Then he let go for an instant and tried to climb up onto the twisting, bouncing hull. He managed to get a foothold on the staves when Hirschfeld slipped back, dropping down into the sea.

Without hesitation Kenny abandoned his precarious footing to dive in after him. The dull greenish water shut off all visibility as he flailed around underwater, trying to grab Hirschfeld. His lungs seemed ready to burst, but still he stayed underwater, kicking his legs, groping with his arms in an effort to find his friend. Just as he was ready to make for the surface his right leg hit something solid. Reaching down with his hand, he felt the slippery surface of the slicker. Seizing hold, he dragged Hirschfeld to the surface.

Water poured from Len's mouth and nose. Kenny knew he could not save Hirschfeld alone. He slammed his open palm across Hirschfeld's face. Len opened dull eyes. "Goddamn you! Fight for your damn life!" Kenny screamed at him.

Hirschfeld's eyes closed. "I can't," he whimpered.

Kenny hit him again, and as he did a wave slammed them against the boat. Hirschfeld wheezed as air was forced from his lungs and greenish vomit poured from his mouth as he threw up the remains of his night of drinking. Kenny dunked Hirschfeld's head into the water, then pulled him up by his hair. Once again he maneuvered him against the side of the boat, then slapped him hard.

"Don't hit me no more, Kenny. No more," Len Hirschfeld begged.

"Climb up there, you mother. Climb up on that thing."

"Jus' lemme go, lemme go."

Kenny smacked him across the mouth again, hating

him. "You friggin' quitter," he screamed. "You don't quit on me! You don't quit!"

"Leave me alone."

Kenny hit him again.

Resignedly, eyes closed, Hirschfeld swung his body around and felt for the rungs of the boat.

Another wave smashed them against the boat. "Try," Kenny screeched. "Try!" Hirschfeld began another half-hearted effort as Kenny shoved him from behind. Kenny's final surge of energy pushed Hirschfeld onto the hull.

Kenny dug his fingers into the wooden sides of the boat and clamored aboard, finally out of the numbing Sound. Temporarily, at least, they were safe. And once again, as in Nam, he was a genuine hero. That thought kept the biting cold at bay.

Shadows ran insanely around the inside of Larry's mind, disappearing before he could determine what they were. He shivered. And yet it was warm and comfortable inside. Then a single thought filled his mind: the gray shepherd.

He opened his eyes and saw a dog. A dog, leaping to kill him. No, no, no. But a dog was there.

"Dopey! Get away!" He closed his eyes and cried.

There was no dial tone. Diane punched at the buttons again, trying to provoke the telephone into life. It was dead. She banged the receiver against the wall in her frustration. At first she did not understand, it had been working well, but as she held the silent receiver to her ear she glanced out the living room window and saw the broken telephone wire lying twisted in the snow.

It was almost funny.

There was nothing to do but wait. She sat near her husband, checking his breathing, waiting for Kenny or the police or the Coast Guard to come bursting out of the woods in the nick of time as would happen on any television show. She considered praying, muttered a few quickly chosen words, but quit in the middle because it somehow made her feel ridiculous.

"How is he?" Frieda's voice startled her. She had almost forgotten there were other people in the house.

"He needs help soon," she said.

"But he'll be all right?" It was not so much a question as a prayer.

The rage within Frieda swelled. The pack had trapped her inside her own home. Her home! It had killed her husband. And now it had done this to her son. They would not have him! She would make sure of that. Dogs would not be allowed to make her a prisoner and force her to watch her son die.

Still wearing her red cloth coat, Frieda Hardman walked past her daughter-in-law, opened the door and stepped out into the yard.

THIRTEEN

Frieda had taken four steps into the yard before Diane realized what was happening. By the time she reached the door there was nothing for her to do but stand and watch in mute horror.

The dogs saw Frieda immediately. The dachshund yapped a metallic threat at her. The dalmatian growled menacingly. But none of the dogs moved toward her. They had first to understand her purpose, to scent her fear.

There was no fear. She was no longer afraid of them. They could do nothing more to frighten her. Driven only by her anger, she walked slowly, almost casually, across the yard.

The shepherd rapidly examined her scents. This was not the enemy, this one was different, the scent was different. And so it held back, thus holding back the pack.

Frieda walked past the burial mound of the Airedale, directly toward the gray dog. She wanted to strike out at it, hurt it, yet she realized that was not her intent. She was going to get the car. The car would save her son's life. She would drive to the front of the house and carry them from the dogs to safety. Later they could deal with the pack.

She passed within five feet of the shepherd, and looked closely at him. The other dogs waited. A short breeze flipped up the collar of her red cloth coat as she moved defiantly through the yard.

The gray dog was bigger than she thought, its pelt still stained with Larry's blood, the gray hair tangled and matted. The dog's mouth hung open and she observed how even its teeth were, gently angled, and sharp. He was a frightening animal, but she was not afraid.

Diane watched in awe as her mother-in-law walked past the pack. For an instant there was no Larry, no pack, only this magnificent old woman.

"Mommy, Mommy, do you know what Corny—" Josh came running into the kitchen.

Diane whirled in alarm. "Shut up!" she whispered.

The boy burst into tears, and Diane went to him, hugging him, than leading him upstairs, afraid his crying would upset the delicate balance in the yard. She got the sobbing child upstairs and returned to the window.

The shepherd moved now, and, for an instant, Diane thought it was going to attack. She stifled a shout of warning. But the dog stopped shifting and stood, its tail held low and stiff, its lips drawn back, trembling ever so slightly, watching the strange figure move toward the bridge.

My son will be saved, Frieda thought. That and nothing else.

The other dogs looked nervously to the shepherd for instructions, but the gray dog stood immobile, watching.

The Chevy coupe stood only a few feet from Frieda, a black lump buried in almost three feet of snowdrifts. Triumphantly she moved closer, still concentrating her thoughts on her son. Six feet. Four feet. The shepherd rose slowly to its feet as Frieda reached the car.

Diane released a long-held breath. Frieda had made it. They would be able to flee to town. Away from the dogs. To telephones. To help. Larry would live. She would get immediate help to the island. If Kenny wasn't there, she would try the police once more. If they wouldn't come when they heard of his injuries she would find somebody who would. For enough money, she knew, she could get help.

She wanted to cry, but tears wouldn't come.

Frieda reached into the pocket of her red cloth coat, groping up for the car keys. At first she did not find them. But they were there. They were always there, tangled in the junk that collected in her pockets. She fingered the various assorted items. A safety pin. Some loose change. She felt the first twinge of apprehension and thrust more deeply into the pocket, searching anxiously. They were not there.

The shepherd began sauntering toward the bridge, his ears perked high with curiosity. The scent in the air was changing.

Get in the car, Diane screamed silently, get in the car!

The keys were not there. They had to be there. Now her search was becoming desperate.

Walking at a steady, almost leisurely pace, the shepherd reached the bridge. Frieda pulled the lining of the pocket inside out, spilling its contents into the snow. A few scraps of paper drifted away even before they hit the ground, but a number of heavier items dropped to the ground. Frieda fell to her knees and scrambled in the snow with her bare hands, searching frantically.

The keys were not there. She knew it with certainty at the same moment Diane realized it. Larry had taken them with him. They were probably still in his bloodstained pocket. Rising, Frieda tried the car door. It would not open. She brushed the snow and caked ice away from the window and looked within. The door did not appear to be locked, but it would not open.

Desperately Frieda yanked at it with all her strength. It did not not move. Beads of sweat broke out on her forehead. Quickly she shuffled around to the other side of the car and tried that door. It was locked.

The shepherd crossed the bridge, lifting its nose, searching out a scent.

Frieda looked around for something to throw at the dog, but she found nothing. She pounded at the car door again, trying to force it open. "No," she screeched at the dog. "No!"

The pack had picked up the scent of her fear. Slowly they moved toward the bridge, a formless mass, bumping and pushing as they crossed it.

Diane tried to think of something to do to distract them, but all she could find in the kitchen were two aluminum pans. Throwing the kitchen door open she ran out into the yard, banging the pans together as hard as she could. "Here! Here!" she cried. The noise temporarily stopped the pack. The shepherd looked back to the house, waiting to see if the sound portended danger.

Frieda struck at the car window with her fists. But the safety glass was much too strong for her. She was still beating at the window when the shepherd decided the clanging was not a threat and moved toward her again.

Twenty yards from the car the dog broke into a trot, smoothly gliding in and out of the snow along the path she'd made. Frieda began backing away from the protection the Chevy gave her, searching for help that was not coming. The shepherd increased its pace, more confident now. Behind the shepherd the pack was closing in.

Frieda turned and began to run, her fear pervading the air, the dogs directly behind her.

The shepherd closed rapidly, his legs churning as he bounded toward her. He hunched down to begin his leap, but before he could catapult himself, he stopped abruptly. The enemy had disappeared.

With a piercing scream, Frieda Hardman tumbled forward into the gorge, dying instantly as her skull smashed against the rocks.

Diane closed and locked the door, then burst into tears. For Frieda and Tom and Larry, but mostly for herself. She was alone, utterly helpless. Frieda was dead, Tom was dead and Larry was dying, and there was nothing she could do about it. Nothing. She needed somebody to tell her what to do, to tell her how to save her own and her children's lives. Where were the police? Where was Kenny? Anybody.

"Diane," Larry whispered painfully.

She wiped hastily at her tears. "Yes, darling?"

His voice was weak. "Need help."

"I know." She raised his head and held it in her lap, gently stroking his hot forehead. "I'll get help."

He swallowed painfully, closing his eyes. "It hurts."

"Try to go to sleep now. I'll get help. I promise, Larry, I'll get help."

Diane was sure he would not be able to sleep. But unless she found a weapon, unless she found a way of getting to the car, he would not live. Be calm, she told herself, look carefully through the house. And think! Use your brains. There's got to be something to fight them with.

Her search began in the kitchen. Methodically Diane went through each cabinet and closet, searched the shelves, peered under the sink. She was not sure what she was looking for but, if it was there, she would find it. There was nothing in the kitchen that might serve as a weapon.

Nor the living room.

Nor the front bedroom. Please let there be another gun hidden away somewhere, she prayed, knowing even as she prayed that no such weapon existed. The back bedroom turned up nothing and she was forced to spend precious minutes there calming Josh and Marcy.

Corny looked up as Diane entered the third bedroom. "Where's Frieda, what have you done with her?" she demanded.

Biting her lip to hold back the tears, Diane lied, "She went away." What she really needed, she thought drastically, was a bomb. Oh, God, where was Kenny?

"But she didn't say good-bye," Corny was protesting sadly.

"She'll be back." There was nothing in that bedroom either.

The patio had been closed off for the winter, so it took some time to get the door open. She found nothing useful there among the wicker summer furniture, a hammock and a small wrought-iron table.

The bathrooms were her last hope. Diane rummaged through the medicine cabinet, dropping everything that was of no use to her on the floor. Soon the shelves were empty. A pile of patent medicine, pills, aspirin, and assorted bottles lay discarded at her feet.

There was nothing in the house that she could use to drive off the dogs. Larry would die.

Abruptly her eyes focused on the single can on the bathroom washbasin. Larry's aerosol shaving cream, sitting right where he left it. She picked it up and held it to her breast, imagining she could still feel the warmth from his hands. This silly can was something he had used. The curve of the can seemed to fit her hand. I'll make something out of this, she promised herself, at least I'll fight them with something.

As she held the can at eye level, she stared at it. One word, in capital letters stood out from the instructions neatly printed on the side. CAUTION.

She read the instructions carefully, realizing this would be her weapon.

The gray shepherd stood on the edge of the gorge looking down at the body spread-eagled on the snow-covered rocks. It did not move, therefore it presented no further threat to the pack. The scent of fear had dissolved on the wind.

A gust of wind swept through the gorge, lifting the collar of the red cloth coat, but as the wind died the collar fell limp and the dogs lost interest. One by one they followed the shepherd back across the bridge. The dachshund was the last to leave, barking a final wild taunt at the lifeless body on the rocks before it turned to go.

At the far end of the bridge the shepherd halted. Was the enemy still alive inside the house? Was it more important to scour the woods for food? Or the house? The pack clustered obediently behind its leader.

There was still time to hunt food, and they must make sure the enemy, the man who killed, was gone. The shepherd turned into the yard.

Kenny watched the stone gray storm clouds rolling overhead. Hirschfeld lay stretched out beside him on the hull, breathing raggedly, his teeth chattering loudly from the cold. Kenny realized his friend was in bad shape. Every few minutes he shook Hirschfeld s arm until he opened his eyes. He could not be allowed to fall asleep. If he slipped into the water again Kenny doubted he had the strength to get him back up on the hull.

Actually, he admitted, he didn't care very much about Leonard Hirschfeld. He was too fat, too slovenly, he'd let himself go to seed. If Hirschfeld didn't care about himself, why should Kenny? Pledge, that was his type of man, strong, quiet, but really smart. When Pledge said something, it made sense. His mind, like his body, tolerated no waste.

Then why the hell had he jumped into the goddamn freezing water and risked his own life to save fat Hirschfeld? He considered that question. Well, he decided, it was what he had to do. That's what the Army taught him, save your buddy's ass. Black or white, fat or thin, everybody had to work together. He didn't mind the thought of being a hero again. That wasn't such a bad thing. There aren't enough real heroes in the world, that's one of the really big problems. Too many pussyfooters. Too many fags. Too many businessmen. Too many Larrys.

Larry was a goddamn wimp! Always playing it safe. Not at all like the old man. The old man was a tough buck. Strong back, solid muscles, close to the land. I'm glad I'm like him, Kenny decided, only then remembering the old man was dead.

That fact really struck him for the first time. It was no longer an intangible thought; it was fact. Dogs had killed the old man. Dogs! It seemed impossible, the old man could handle dogs like Evel Knievel could handle a bike. The old man, dead! Murdered by dogs? Not goddamn likely. He'd seen a lot of people get it in Nam, in all sorts of gruesome ways, but those had all been faceless beings in dirty khaki fatigues. And always the other guy. This was different. This was family. His own flesh. This reminder of his own mortality struck him hard, and frightened him.

Yards away from the boat the first yellow slicker seemed to reappear magically. Kenny watched it as a gentle ripple picked it up, partially revealing the gasoline can floating underneath. So that was what first bumped the boat, Kenny thought.

He shook Len's arm. That gas can saved your life, Hirschfeld, he thought, that stupid tin can kept you alive.

Kenny could not tear his mind away from thoughts of his own death.

Now that she had a plan, a plan to destroy the pack, Diane raced through the house gathering the necessary components for her weapon. In the second bathroom she found a bottle of rubbing alcohol, a can of spray deodorant and a can of foot powder, all of which she put with the green shaving can. In one of the bedrooms she discovered a pink aerosol can of hairspray. The kitchen yielded two cans of lighter fluid, two cans of spot remover and an aerosol spray cleaner. And on the porch she struck a bonanza: two pints of blue paint, a can containing paint thinner and another turpentine.

The thought of the weapon possessed her; she pictured it in her mind as she worked briskly. It was amazing, she thought, what you could do with simple everyday household supplies. She took several jars of Frieda Hardman's home-preserved fruits, opened them, and emptied the contents into the sink. The jars were vital pieces of equipment.

Finished with her collecting, Diane took one of Larry's best dress shirts, she had no idea why he'd packed such an expensive shirt for this trip to this island, and ripped it into shreads. Then she set all her materials on the kitchen table and began constructing her weapon. A regular Park Avenue radical, she thought, and the thought made her smile shakily. But if the various warnings on the labels were accurate, these junkyard bombs would save their lives.

She placed a spray can and a mixture of her various fuels into each canning jar, then attached a strip of shirt cloth to each jar as a fuse. She added a smattering of nails and screws and bolts she'd discovered in a cabinet to each jar. Finally she tried to screw the tops back onto the jars.

She couldn't quite get the tops screwed on, the cloth fuses preventing the lids from catching the proper grooves. After puzzling over the problem briefly, she took a can opener and punched a single hole in the top of each lid. The hole proved just large enough to allow her to pull the makeshift fuse through. It might not be the right way to do it, she decided, but it made the most sense.

Besides, the odds against the jars actually exploding, and hurting the dogs if they did, were fantastically high. There was nothing to lose.

She placed the bombs on the kitchen table in a neat line. They looked almost pretty. Like a picture in the housewares section of a Bloomingdale's catalogue. "Bombs for the home," she said aloud, "for the family that has everything." Including a pack of murderous dogs in the front yard.

The best way to deliver them would be to throw them as far as she could, into the middle of the pack. Then, what? Wait, of course. If they did explode there would be plenty of time to bring the children and Corny downstairs again. And if they did not. . . . She cut off the thought.

One by one, she transferred the bombs to the floor next to the kitchen door, then carefully wet their cloth fuses with lighter fluid. She opened the door slightly and looked outside. The boxer was lying on its side in the snow no more than thirty feet from the door. The lean Irish setter sat beside him, busily cleaning itself. Behind them the dachshund circled nervously. A few yards further on the Labrador and a painfully thin dalmatian sat side by side in the snow. A wolfhound lay apparently asleep a few yards from the bridge, and near him the collie determinedly scratched behind its ear. The other dogs were scattered about the yard. Overseeing them all, far off to the right, almost hidden under the wooden fence that protected the gorge, lay the shepherd.

The shepherd watched with rising interest as the kitchen door opened, slightly at first, then halfway. Was it the enemy again? Perking up his ears, he rose to his haunches, facing the house, straining to pick up warning sounds.

Diane struck a wooden match and lit the first makeshift fuse. It caught immediately, burning even more quickly than she had supposed it would. In one easy motion she flipped the jar out into the yard. It clumped to earth near the setter and rolled a few feet before stopping. Nervously the boxer got to its feet and moved away.

The shepherd watched as the brief flame lit up the kitchen shadows. A scent of burning sulphur drifted to him. Emitting a single sharp bark of warning, he started moving farther away from the house. Slowly, almost lazily, as the tranquilizers in the food finally began to affect them, the other dogs began moving.

Diane lit each of the remaining jars as rapidly as she could. As soon as each fuse caught she threw the jar into the yard, aiming them in different areas, trying to throw them high enough so they would carry well away from the house but low enough so they would not smash on impact. Two of the jars ended up within inches of each other, and another fell into a hole in the snow and disappeared, but the rest ended up well distributed throughout the yard.

The fuse burned well in the first canning jar. But then it sizzled, popped, and died. The jar filled with smoke but did not even crack.

That's only one, Diane thought optimistically, just one.

Then she draped her body over Larry, keeping her weight on her hands and knees, and waited for an explosion.

Outside, the dachshund, ignoring the shepherd's warning, trotted over to inspect one of the jars. He sniffed at the jar containing the aerosol hairspray and a heavy mixture of lighter fluid and blue paint.

Sniffing it, the dog cocked his head as a hissing sound came from within. He turned as if to signal the pack that these things were harmless, but before he could bark, the bomb blew him apart.

Only four of the jars actually exploded, but they were enough. The force of the explosions splintered the jars into hundreds of tiny fragments, and blasted these razor-sharp fragments into the air with deadly effect. Larger pieces of glass together with the nails, screws and bolts shot through the air like misshapen bullets, ripping into anything they struck. The dachshund died in the initial explosion. The boxer took four or five pieces of glass and metal in his body, but managed to scramble to the protection of the woods. A single nail caught the Irish setter in the back of the skull and it thrashed around awkwardly before dying. A razor-sharp metal fragment of tin from the foot spray can ripped into the wolfhound, tearing a bloody hole in its gut. Life, death or injury depended completely on luck. The dalmatian had half its skull sliced off by a flying chunk of glass. The Labrador, next to him, was untouched. The surviving dogs turned and fled into the forest.

As the homemade bombs detonated, the sound of the explosions, pieces of metal and shattered glass ricocheting against the house, told Diane they had been destructive. Rising to her feet, she ran to the kitchen window in time to see the frightened survivors fleeing over the bridge. From inside, though, it was difficult to see exactly how much damage had been done. The kitchen window itself was cobwebbed by connecting cracks, although it had not broken.

Satisfied there were no living dogs still near the house, Diane cautiously opened the kitchen door to look out upon the carnage. There were splotches of blood in several portions of the yard. Bits of blue paint spotted the snow, the fence, and the side of the house. The carcass of the Irish setter lay in the middle of the yard, not far from the twisted remains of the dalmatian. The dying wolfhound, baying its pain, limped across the bridge, leaving a trail of blood behind. But she could not locate the shepherd.

And then it was there.

The big gray dog sat in the far corner of the yard by the fence, staring at her. From where she was Diane could not see if it was hurt, although there seemed to be blood on its coat. There was no way of knowing if the blood was its own, another dog's or Larry's. She stood, watching the leader of the pack, waiting for it to move.

The shepherd had almost reached the bridge when the first jar exploded and he stood transfixed, bewildered, watching helplessly as his pack was blown apart. A thin scrap of tin had scored his back, and although it burned him badly, it was largely a superficial wound.

The shepherd made no attempt to halt the escape of the surviving dogs across the bridge. Instead he waited, alone, in the yard. All that was left was the enemy.

He saw the figure standing in the doorway as a mixture of dull grays and blacks. The dog could not focus well, the daylight was too bright and the tranquilizers had affected his already poor vision, but what was left of his other senses told him that this was a new enemy.

Tiredly, the shepherd rose and began moving slowly around the yard, inspecting the remains of his pack. He sniffed at the body of the setter, then pushed at it with a paw. Standing over the dalmatian, he pawed at its headless body, then kicked at the bloodied snow.

Diane closed and bolted the door, then jammed a kitchen chair underneath the knob. The shepherd could not get into the house.

Then she watched from the shattered window as the solitary figure moved about the yard, sniffing, searching. It did not seem possible that the dog would remain, but it did. And as long as it stayed in the yard there was no safe way to get to the car. Somehow, she realized, she would have to meet this dog alone and destroy it.

FOURTEEN

Once again Diane ransacked the kitchen, searching now for a smaller weapon that she could use against the shepherd. The success of the canning-jar bombs had given her confidence in her own abilities. She no longer needed anyone else. It was just a matter of staying calm, looking carefully, thinking intelligently, and utilizing the everyday household materials that sat tantalizingly in front of her eyes.

What is there in the house that's dangerous? she wondered. What things did she make sure the maid kept away from the children? Poisons. Acids. Sharp objects. Detergents. She knew she was on the right track, so she sifted again through all the boxes and bottles in the cabinets and closets, looking for a practical weapon. Nothing seemed right. Then, buried under the sink, next to the pipes, she found it. The ultimate weapon. And even better, in using it, she could turn the dog's hatred to her own advantage. She would make him an offering, then destroy him with it.

Larry's pulse seemed regular and his breath steady. He even seemed to be a little stronger. As carefully as possible, she dug into his pants pocket and withdrew the keys to the Chevy. They were covered with dried blood, and she held them by their tips as she washed them clean. Then, leaning down over her husband, she spoke in his ear. "Are you awake?"

He made a sound.

"If I help you, do you think you can make it to the door?" she asked.

The tip of his tongue crept out from between dry lips to lick them. "Yes," he whispered hoarsely. "Yes."

Diane kissed him, then went upstairs. The explosions had frightened both children and they were still crying. "Listen," she demanded as she tried to comfort them, "do you want to go home?"

"Yes." Josh pouted through his tears.

"I wanna go home, Mommy," Marcy wailed loudly.

"We'll go soon. But you both have to stay here until I come and get you. Don't either of you dare come out of this room until Mommy comes for you, okay?" Eventually the police would arrive at the house, so even if she did not make it to the car, the children would still be safe. But she would make it. There was no longer any doubt in her mind.

"Is Dopey coming too?" Josh asked.

The little dog sat in the corner, happily wagging his tail. As Diane looked at his small, loving face, a chill ran through her. She wondered if she would ever be able to touch that dog again. "Of course," she assured them. "Of course Dopey's coming home with us."

After stopping in the front bedroom to collect the last of Larry's shirts, she went into Cornelia's room. The old woman was sitting in a rocking chair, softly singing what sounded to Diane like a hymn. Diane left the room and went back downstairs to the kitchen. Pulling a large dirty pot from the sink, she began to prepare her weapon for the final encounter.

Len Hirschfeld started sliding from the hull. The storm seemed to be abating, but the cold was as intense as ever. His fingers scrabbled at the lapstrake, but he could not maintain his hold on the slick wood. "Help me, Kenny," he screamed.

"Hold on, Len," Kenny shouted back. The choppy seas battering the hull made it all but impossible to help.

"I'm slipping, Kenny, I'm slipping. Help me, please, help me," Len pleaded.

Kenny reached across the hull as best he could, trying to grasp Hirschfeld without endangering his own precarious hold. But, fully extended, his reach was inches short.

Slowly, almost gracefully, like a bloated tanker sliding down the wales, Len Hirschfeld slid off the hull into the green water. His single scream was shut off by a crashing wave. He floated by a few feet from Kenny, and for one instant Kenny again had the option of risking his own life to try and save Hirschfeld's. The remembrance flashed through his mind of how he'd leaped into the open to pull two buddies from the flames of a Vietnam firefight.

But that had been so long ago. Before death struck so closely.

He held onto the hull tightly, crying out in frustration, "I can't, Len, I can't. I can't." The last Kenny saw of Hirschfeld was a fat hand clawing desperately at the water. Then he was gone.

He held on, held on with both hands, tearing at the wood with his short fingernails, digging in as the sea tried to tear him from the hull, but he would not loose his grip. His eyes stung badly and the salt water had cracked his lips, but he was still alive, and he would not surrender to the sea.

Instead he forced himself to focus his thoughts on his brother. I tried, Larry, he screamed silently, I swear it, I tried to help you.

All that was left now was survival. Then he would explain everything to Larry, make him understand. An image of their father, sitting in the old brown easy chair, puffing on the Christmas present pipe, fled through his mind. It's not my fault, I didn't let him down. I didn't let anyone down. That image was replaced by a second: Len Hirschfeld's fat hand clutching at the hull.

Another wave crashed down on the hull and opened a long crack between the keel and the lapstrake sides. Kenny watched the water as it drained through the opening into the interior of the hull.

Sergeant Stewart Stromfeld stretched, yawned, and finally lifted his body from the vinyl chair to greet Sergeant Peter Dichter, his friend but, much more important, his replacement. "Am I late?" Dichter joked.

"Two ass-kissing days," Stromfeld told him. The captain discouraged vulgarity in the station house, but this was a special occasion. Now he could sleep.

Stromfeld filled Dichter in as rapidly as he could, visions of the cot in the back cell filling his head. "The Coast Guard just about cleaned up the freighter mess, and they're on a sweep looking for small craft in trouble. When they check back in, tell 'em we got a Mayday from Burrows Island. . . ." He briefly told his replacement of the telephone calls.

"Dogs, huh?" Dichter said, shaking the snow off his uniform jacket.

"That's what they said. Dogs."

"It's a crazy world."

Stromfeld agreed.

They ruffled the papers that had to be ruffled, signed the proper records, and Dichter eased his baby-faced bulk into the vinyl chair. "Hey, Stromfeld," he called, stopping the sergeant in the hallway, "I got one for you."

"Yeah? What's that?"

"How does the guy who drives the snow plow get to the snow plow?" He laughed.

"Go screw yourself," Stromfeld told him good-naturedly as he went through the door.

Left alone, Dichter began reassembling Stromfeld's papers into neat, efficient piles. In a few hours, when the storm passed, when the Coast Guard made contact, or when the police department got its own launch out there, he would see that one of them made Burrows Island the first stop. "Dogs," he muttered aloud, "dogs?"

Diane dipped the last of Larry's shirts into the pool of blood that had collected under her husband's right arm. Then she took the almost-full bottle of household lye and poured it into the dirty pot. A present for the shepherd.

Armed once again, she opened the door and walked out into the yard.

The dog moved nervously across her path. But he kept his distance, wary of the interloper.

Shivering, Diane walked boldly forward in the snow. Be calm, she warned herself, calm. It was no shame, she realized, to lack Frieda Hardman's courage. The pot of lye wobbled uneasily in her right hand, the bloody shirt was extended in her left. "Here, dog," she said sweetly, showing the shirt, "this is for you."

The pot grew heavier and her nervous gait caused it to swirl. A few drops flew over the lip and burned her hand. She did not notice. "Come and see what I have for you, come here now," she cajoled softly.

The shepherd backed away cautiously. The mixture of scents in the air confused him. Not one, but two. And the thick scent of blood. The dog tried to sort the different scents out, but it was proving difficult.

"Don't run away, dog. Come over to me. Come to me," Diane begged.

The dog stopped. The soothing voice interested him. He stood his ground, waiting as the figure walked closer. She was ten yards away, then seven.

The shepherd began closing. One step, two. He stopped again, sniffed, took another step forward. Now the bloody scent was clear. It emerged from the other scents and took over. This was her offering. He gathered for a leap, launching himself into the air, straight at Diane.

As the dog sprang, Diane heaved the contents of the pot at his head. Lye splattered across his face, burning into his eyes and mouth. The shepherd dropped to the ground and began frantically clawing at its eyes. He rolled in the wet snow, trying to wash the searing fluid from them.

Diane didn't wait to see the results of her toss. As soon as she threw the lye she dropped the pot and raced for the car, not even hesitating to look back to see if the dog was behind her. With each step she expected to feel its weight on her back. But the dog did not come, and she reached the car.

Calm. Calm. Repeating that word over and over, she slipped what she hoped was the right key into the door lock and turned it. She tugged at the door, breaking loose the ice that encrusted it, and the door finally opened. She scrambled inside, slamming the door shut, locking it from inside, knocking more snow and ice from the windows.

And then she sat shaking in the front seat of the car, her eyes closed, trying to calm her pounding heart. I made it, she thought gratefully, I made it! The shepherd was nowhere in sight, but its howls of agony registered in her mind, telling her the lye had served its purpose; they were safe. They would be back in their apartment within hours.

After giving her nervous hands time to stop shaking, Diane reached down to put the key in the ignition. The shepherd leaped against the car window. His blood-splotched head was inches from her own, separated only by the thin pane of safety glass. Again, and again, he threw his massive body against the window! The keys fell from her fingers onto the floor as she cowered across the seat. The dog's powerful forelegs slammed into the glass, but still he was not able to break through.

Diane looked directly into the slobbering mouth; the dog bared its fangs.

And then, as suddenly as the dog had appeared, it was gone. The barking ceased. Diane sat up slowly in the driver's seat.

And then another crash against the side of the car sent her sprawling back instinctively. Then minutes dragged by with no sound from outside. It's too strong, the car is too strong, Diane thought, he can't get at me. He's given up. This time she stayed on the passenger side of the front seat, raising up on her knees to look outside. The shepherd was rolling in the snow near the edge of the gorge, pawing at its eyes. Now Diane could hear its whines of pain.

The dog rolled closer to the gorge, seemingly oblivious to its existence. Then a few feet from the edge, the dog stopped and looked toward the house.

Diane followed its line of vision. Corny was standing in the kitchen door, holding Josh with her left hand and Marcy with her right.

Obviously slowed by its pain, and drawn completely by new scents, the shepherd started weaving its way back into the yard.

Diane reached for the keys on the floor and tried to shove one into the ignition. It would not go in. She tried to push the key in by sheer force, but she couldn't make it fit. Calm! She took the second key and tried it in the ignition. It slid in and turned.

Calm! Diane pressed on the gas pedal, driving it to the floor, maniacally trying to pump life into the cold engine. It coughed, caught once, died, caught again, then shuddered dead. The smell of gasoline flooded the car. Start, she begged, please start.

The shepherd had managed to cross the bridge and was making his way painfully toward Corny and the two children.

"Start! Start!" Diane screamed aloud, as she pumped desperately.

The dog was halfway across the yard. A dull rumbling sound came from deep in its throat.

Diane pushed the accelerator all the way to the floor and turned the key. The engine churned heavily, then caught. Diane nursed the engine carefully, desperately trying to urge the car to life.

The shepherd paused to look back over the fence at the black car.

She shifted into drive and the rear wheels spun, but the car did not move. Calm! She shifted into reverse and let the car rock back, then quickly put it into forward again. Then reverse. The car rocked forward and back, then shuddered and burst free.

Sweat was pouring from her now, plastering her hair to her forehead. As she reached the narrow wooden bridge she wiped it from her eyes. Watching the dog as best she could through the ice still covering the windshield, she drove over the creaking bridge into the yard.

Once she felt the rear wheels again on solid ground, Diane pushed the accelerator pedal to the floor. The rear tires slipped, spun, but then caught, and the car picked up speed as it moved across the yard. She aimed directly at the shepherd.

The gray dog was confused by the roaring sound behind him. At the last possible instant he turned to see the black monster bearing down on him and leaped aside.

And almost made it. The front bumper caught the dog's hindquarters, sending him sprawling to the ground.

The pain was incredible. His rear legs would not move. But still he would not stop. Using his front legs, he dragged his shattered body toward the car.

From the edge of the forest the Labrador heard the strange sounds in the yard. The leader, no, no longer the leader, but another dog, the shepherd, had been wounded. Two of the dogs stirred as if to return to the yard, but the Labrador stepped in front to halt them. Once he was sure of his control, the dark dog turned and trotted deeper into the woods. After a moment's hesitation, the remainder of the pack followed him.

Diane jumped from the car a split second after it hit the shepherd. She did not bother looking for the injured dog; if he was not dead, he was surely badly hurt, no longer a menace. She screamed at Corny, "Get them in the car! Josh, get in! Get in!"

Larry's eyes were open and he was trying to lift himself onto his left elbow when she raced into the kitchen. Wordlessly, she moved behind him, helping him get to his feet. He leaned heavily on her as she half dragged, half pulled him to the car. Somehow, later Diane would not be able to remember how, she managed to get him sprawled onto the rear seat.

The shepherd was yelping in pain as he dragged his crippled body toward the car. Diane started to back up, but saw that the dog was still coming after them. She smiled sardonically, then put the Chevy into drive.

The dog saw the car coming at him but there was no way he could move out of its path. It struck him, passing over his body with a soft thump.

Diane drove the car another thirty feet before she slammed on the brakes, almost throwing Larry to the floor. She put the car into reverse and deliberately backed it over the already-dead dog. Stopping, she shifted gears and once again drove over the lifeless body. After which she swung the car around in a wide arc and drove slowly over the bridge.

Safe, she thought, safe, safe, safe, safe, safe. Tears of relief flowed down her cheeks as she drove away from the house.

Hearing the car pull away, Dopey Dog ran down the stairs, through the kitchen and out into the yard. He watched as the car faded into the distance, then loosed a long, lonely howl.

Kenny clung precariously to the boat as it sank lower in the water, his body so numb from the cold that he could no longer feel anything. He wondered how much longer he could hold on. "Forever!" he screamed to no one.

The clouds were lighter now, as if the storm was passing out to sea. As it swept away, the Sound laid still, and a beautiful post-rainstorm lull set in. The waves barely reached his shoulders, now no longer breaking over his head.

Kenny threw up, watching the vomit drift inland with the current.

With the last of his strength, he lifted his right leg onto the lapstrake hull and tried to climb higher out of the water. But he no longer had the strength to pull himself to the top. For a moment he hung onto the hull, the lower half of his numb body in the water, swearing softly to himself that he would never, ever, let go.

Then he fell back into the water, sinking quickly below the surface.

EPILOGUE

The *Bountiful Islander* was crammed with television sets, suitcases, hammocks, linens, food, men, women, cats, canaries, and summer dogs as it pulled to the dock this first sunny Saturday in May.

"Bring the dog," the father ordered, "and make sure you keep him on his leash."

"Can you carry everything, dear?" the mother asked, picking up her shoulder bag and magazines. "Need any help?"

He hoisted the two suitcases. "No, I can do it."

Their red wagon was waiting chained to the railing at the dock where it had been left to rust the previous September, and they filled it with the first of their summer possessions. Each weekend there would be additional bundles, until the house was finally filled. The parties would start at the end of the month, and by June the mother would be settled in for the summer. The father would make the trip on weekends until his vacation in late July, when he would join them for three weeks.

The summer would pass quickly and there would be laughs, and sunburns, and happy times, and by summer's end they would pride themselves on their tanned and healthy bodies. Sometime in August a whale would surface off the beach, attracting wide attention. Later that same month a summer visitor's wedding would be held in the carefully decorated town hall.

In the woods, barely aware of the activity on the dock, was a small terrier who had once been named Dopey, but who now lived in the woods and ran with the pack.